▫HOME BOY▫

Also by Joyce Hansen

THE GIFT-GIVER

HOME BOY

◻ ◼ ◻ ◼ ◻

JOYCE HANSEN

CLARION BOOKS
NEW YORK

Clarion Books
a Houghton Mifflin Company imprint
215 Park Avenue South, New York, NY 10003
Text copyright © 1982 by Joyce Hansen
All rights reserved.
For information about permission to reproduce
selections from this book, write to Permissions,
Houghton Mifflin Company,
215 Park Avenue South, New York, NY 10003.
Printed in the USA

Library of Congress Cataloging in Publication Data
Hansen, Joyce. Home boy.

Summary: As he seeks a place to hide, Marcus, a boy from
the Islands now living in the Bronx, tries to figure out how
he became involved in the stabbing of a fellow student.
[1. Bronx (New York, N.Y.)—Fiction] I. Title.
PZ7.H19825Ho   [Fic]   82-1303
ISBN 0-89919-114-2 PA ISBN 0-395-69625-9

AGM 10 9 8 7 6 5 4

For my grandmothers, Amy and Viola,
and for June, Maxwell, and Brenda

□ 1 □

Marcus watched Cassandra as she stared out the bus window. He wanted to say something, but only his grandmother's words came to mind: "You the kind of person who have to be burned before he believe the fire is hot." He held Cassandra's hand tightly and twisted nervously in his seat. The bus crawled up Crotona Avenue. It seemed to him that at least twenty people boarded at every stop.

Marcus dreaded going to school and at the same time he couldn't wait to get there. Everyone would be surprised. He had his books, he'd go to all of his classes, and he had no more joints to sell. He'd also have to inform people that he was no longer Jamaica, but Marcus Bates again.

"Jamaica" was the nickname they'd given him over eighteen months ago when he first came to Langston High School in the Bronx. Marcus had just then arrived from St. Cruz, a small Caribbean island most people had never heard of. Jamaica seemed to be the only island Americans knew about, and when anyone heard Marcus speak they immediately assumed he was from Jamaica. He didn't mind the name then.

Marcus rubbed Cassandra's soft, dark hand. How did she do it, he wondered. She'd made it to her senior year, passed all of her subjects, and stayed out of trouble. Maybe it was easier for girls.

1

Cassandra turned away from the window. "What's wrong, Marcus?"

"Nothing."

"You nervous? Still thinking about that mess?"

Marcus put his arms around her shoulders. "I all right. Sometimes at night I think I can still hear John scream and the shots. But it was school I was thinking about. I wasted almost two years . . . you know I . . ."

"You can do it, Marcus. Maybe the years wasn't wasted because you learned what you need to be about."

"You think everything go' be just fine because I decide to change? Soon as I walk in there somebody go' ask me to sell them a joint."

"So. You ain't selling anymore."

"It seem useless, Cassie. I so far behind. I like a caveman and everyone else in the space age."

Cassandra laughed and Marcus felt a little easier. He almost suggested that they forget about school and spend the whole day alone with each other. Then the nervousness would leave. The fear of not being able to return to school as a different person would disappear. He'd forget about John, the drug dealer he had worked for. But he couldn't suggest that. He had to prove to himself, to Cassie, to his mother and grandmother that he'd finally learned that the fire was hot.

They got off the bus at Fordham Road and walked arm in arm to the side entrance of the school. Cassandra looked at her watch. "We're almost late for homeroom. You better not walk me to my room."

"Okay, Cassie . . . I . . ."

She put her arm lightly around his waist. "Hey, just stay calm. You can make it, Marcus. See you later."

He watched her run up the stairs. Ordinarily he would've

2

He only meant to scare Eddie. Eddie backed away from Marcus as he laughed. "Put that nail file away. You don't have the guts to use it. The only thing you could be is a pusher, and now you even afraid to do that!"

It was as if Eddie had pulled the scab off an old wound and exposed raw flesh. Marcus couldn't contain his fury. When he plunged the blade into Eddie's stomach it felt like the pulp of a soft plum. The laughter of the crowd turned to screams.

Eddie fell backward, into the throng of screaming students. A girl shouted, "He's dead!" Marcus ran.

He wanted to go to the bathroom but his legs had their own will. They ran. He didn't remember tearing down the stairs and past the school guard, nor did he know how he got to the subway. He wanted to reach down in his pocket and show his train pass. His feet wouldn't let him. They jumped over the turnstile. A train pulled into the station and he darted in.

His heart beat wildly, as if it would tear his chest wide open. His mouth was dry. The car was almost empty. He sat down and buried his head in his chest. His mind was in little pieces.

He was afraid to look at his trembling hands. It felt as if they still held the knife. He was afraid that if he looked at them he'd see two bloody things. Marcus folded his arms across his chest and balled his fists in an attempt to stop the shaking.

The train pulled away from the station and Marcus looked to see where he was. But in a split second he'd forgotten what he saw; his mind was too shattered now to focus on anything. The trembling stopped and he stared at his hands. They were the same. He turned them over. There was no blood on his palms. Nothing.

The train stopped at another station and about forty elementary school students came running in screaming. The adults with them yelled and pushed the children into seats. Marcus slowly raised his head. The noise and confusion reminded him of his first day at Langston High School almost two years ago.

□ 2 □

When he walked into the classroom that first day of school fifteen pairs of eyes watched his white shirt that had gone limp from too many washings and his light blue polyester pants that squeezed his buttocks and thighs before flaring out over the pointed toes of his shoes. One very pretty dark-skinned girl gave him the only friendly smile he got that day.

The teacher looked up from a pile of papers on her desk. Marcus's hand shook slightly as he handed her his program card.

"My name is Mrs. Schwartz, Marcus," the teacher said. "This will be your homeroom and mathematics class. The bell's going to ring shortly and you can go to your next class."

"Thank you, Miss," he said in a sing-song voice that came out too shrill. Someone snickered. The teacher's head shot up. She sat Marcus in the back of the room with two other big boys. One of them slept with his head on the desk. The other boy stared at Marcus as if were seeing something from another world. A third boy, with red specks in his eyes, stood in the doorway. He grinned at Marcus and called out something to the other two boys before he walked away.

These boys want to give me a good lashing, Marcus

thought. He barely understood the teacher, even though she spoke English. The accent was so different, it sounded to him like someone speaking a foreign language through her nose.

Marcus didn't want to move, to turn, to think. They'd all see him. A bell rang and everyone scrambled. He wished he could stay in that room for the entire first day—stay there until he became more accustomed to things. The teacher frowned at him. "Hurry, Marcus. Don't move so slowly. You'll miss your next class."

Hurry to where? he thought.

Marcus walked slowly out of the room. A boy kicked a girl in her back and she ran down the hall roaring after him. People seemed to be sliding and knocking their way from one end of the hall to the other.

One wall was filled with brilliantly colored graffiti. Marcus stopped for a moment to try to make some sense out of it. "The Kings of 175th." "Duke." "Killer 157." Marcus never forgot that wall. Wherever he saw graffiti it reminded him of New York City and those first, lonely, frightening days at school.

Marcus continued down the hall and thought about the school back home. There everyone dressed in white shirts and blouses and blue pants and skirts. Green lizards crawled up the building, and Mr. Blakey, the teacher, stood in front of the school with his big, brown pants blowing in the morning breeze—his glasses making two silver spots on his round, dark cheeks. Marcus felt a dull pain he couldn't identify. Here there were so many rooms, students, teachers. No one paid any attention to him in the halls. He could have been a speck on the wall.

Someone looked over his shoulder at the program card he carried. "Twinkle Toes, you supposed to be in this room." It was the red-eyed boy. Marcus said nothing. He walked into the class and sat in front, hoping the teacher wouldn't make him move to the back of the room. Marcus saw that the teacher didn't even seem to know he was a new student. A wad of paper bounded off his head. Someone yelled, "Let's hear some calypso talk."

Marcus's temple pulsed. He turned around. The same three boys were in the back of the room. "What you looking at?" one of them yelled. He seemed to be drunk or high. The red-eyed boy laughed.

"Please stop. That's not nice," the teacher said. Marcus thought about what he'd do if he were back home. He'd get his best friend, Sellie, and the two Duncan brothers and they'd tear these boys apart. He had no partners now.

Another wad of paper flew past his head. The teacher stood up timidly. "Now class, please." Marcus discovered that the class belonged to the students. He turned around to the back of the room again. A little, short girl filed her fingernails. The red-eyed boy read the newspaper, while his two friends talked and laughed. Two Spanish boys practiced dance steps. Marcus laughed to himself. Wait till I write Sellie and them about this crazy place. You can do whatever you want here.

Marcus laughed out loud this time. The teacher looked frightened and the other students seemed surprised. "That new boy's off," someone said. The teacher said something. The red-eyed boy told the teacher to go to hell and stalked out of the room. Marcus was given a thick history book. A girl screamed. The teacher screamed back and wrote something on a piece of paper. Then she told the class that they would see a film.

Something was wrong with the projector. Everyone's attention was on either fixing it or making insulting remarks to the teacher. Marcus relaxed a little and looked around the

9

room. One wall was lined with clothing closets. The teacher attempted to decorate the drab gray-green walls with colorful posters from various countries. There was a smiling blond face from Sweden; the Eiffel Tower; Big Ben in London; and two large maps of Europe and the United States. The blackboard in front of the room was covered with writing, and a heavy odor of chalk, stale sweat, and age hung over the entire room.

When the projector was repaired someone turned off the lights and the bell rang. A boy yelled, "I want my money back. What kind of movie is this?" Everyone tumbled out of the room. Marcus was pushed into another room that happened to be the right class.

The teacher looked harassed. His thick glasses seemed to fog over as soon as the students walked in. He tried to smile at Marcus, but it was obvious that the thought of processing a new student in his class unnerved him. "I'll give you your books and a test tomorrow, so I can see where you fit in."

Marcus almost laughed in his face. He'd never heard such a strange sounding voice. It was like a rusty machine.

Marcus felt as if he were outside of himself; that he was suspended somewhere in the room, looking at what was happening. He didn't write anything, open a book, or listen to what the teacher said. No one asked him to, so he sat and waited for the bell to ring.

At three o'clock he walked quickly to the bus stop. Some of the students glanced his way, but most ignored him. The large group of kids at the bus stop looked like troops in formation ready to advance in his direction. He walked home. It was about a mile from the school to 179th Street where he lived.

He walked up Fordham Road to Crotona Avenue and had an imaginary conversation with Sellie and the Duncan brothers. Sellie would look at the old tenement on the corner and say, "Is this America? Miss Lorna grass roof look better than that building." Dudley Duncan would say, "But look. So many stores. So much to buy." David Duncan would say, "I love these girls. They is looking fine. I want to buy or steal one of them."

They'd laugh all the way home, and Marcus would feel as if he belonged somewhere. He was a little calmer, but then he saw a tall, straight old black woman walking toward him.

The woman stared at him with heavily lidded eyes that gave her a haughty expression—his grandmother's eyes. Marcus smiled at her and would have liked to tell her how much she looked like his grandmother. She gripped her shopping bag tightly, and Marcus saw fear in her eyes as she passed him. He only wanted to say something to her—some little thing. Instead he watched the taunting vision of his dead grandmother walk away from him and fought tears the rest of the way home.

Marcus reached for the small black-and-white television as soon as he entered the apartment. This was the only thing he liked about America—the little square screen that had shows all day and night. The family couldn't afford a television back home, and even if they could, the station didn't have programs for twenty-four hours.

Marcus sprawled across the sagging couch and entered the world of "I Love Lucy" and "The Flintstones." The first day at school was forgotten. He loved the way television wiped out everything from his head. He didn't have to think about anything until his father came home.

Marcus didn't realize his father was in the apartment until he heard him suck his teeth loudly. He hadn't even heard him put the key in the door. "Damn, I tired. Your mother home yet?"

Rudolph Bates was a handsome, stocky man. His steel gray Afro accentuated his full, strong features. He and Marcus had the same reddish brown skin and amber eyes. "Tell your mother to wake me so I can eat before I go to work."

"Yes." Marcus would have liked to talk about his first day at school, but that would have to wait until his mother came home. He only talked to his father when it was absolutely necessary. Marcus returned to the television.

About half an hour later his mother came home from work. She sat down wearily and slipped off her brown loafers. "Marcus? You fall asleep in front the television?"

"Hello, Mommy."

"Is this what you do all day?"

"What else is there to do?"

"You ain't see this house need a little dusting and sweeping? You ain't have no homework? I come home and you lounging like you have maid and butler. I get paid to be a nursemaid to them two brats, but I ain't coming home to be nursemaid to no boy big as you." She folded her arms and threw her legs out in front of her.

"Mommy, why you fighting me? I ain't even have a book, much less homework. Just one big history book, and the house look clean to me." He went over to her and sat on the arm of the chair. "I miss home. It so strange here."

Her face softened and the hard lines around her mouth disappeared into a smile. She rubbed his arm. "Marcus, you get used to this place. Someday we go home again. School is always hard the first day or so. By tomorrow you get books and homework."

While he watched her prepare supper, Marcus felt that he was part of his surroundings for the first time that day. He didn't want to spoil the feeling by talking about school again. The smell of garlic, onions, and peppers reminded him of home and of his grandmother. If he mentioned his grandmother his mother would begin to cry. Since what he felt couldn't be expressed in words he said, "Daddy say to wake him so he could eat before he go to work. He don't have the porter job in the hospital anymore?"

"Yes. He have two jobs now. He just started driving a taxi at night. The poor man is always tired."

And evil, Marcus thought.

Marcus and his father had come to New York together that July, but even during the airplane flight they had barely spoken to each other. Louisa, Marcus's mother, had arrived in the city the year before. She took care of two children during the day and cleaned in an office building at night. There were five other children in the family who would be sent for later.

The food didn't taste as good to Marcus as it had smelled. His father looked as if he were too tired to talk and his mother seemed too tired to care. Marcus stared at his plate. So much food—plantain, green salad, codfish cakes, rice, rolls, and juice. A meal back home was usually just rice and fish, or red bean soup with plantain and bread. Sometimes they'd have a piece of beef or pork. Big meals like this were only for special occasions.

If they were back home his sisters and brothers would be there. One of his father's many friends would be around also. Rudy would sit at the head of the table and tell some crazy story, like the time Miss Sara kept baking even though a hurricane had blown the roof off the house.

An old neighborhood woman everyone called Aunty often visited during the evening meal. She'd say, "Oh God, If I know you was eating I come some other time."

"It's nothing, Aunty, have some food with us," his mother always answered.

13

"No child, I just ate me supper. But I'll take a piece of plantain to keep all you company." Aunty would end up with an entire plate of food; it had become a mealtime ritual.

Marcus never thought he could miss those times and people—especially an old fixture like Aunty. They were just everyday parts of his world then, like the plum trees and the azure skies. But enclosed in that cramped kitchen in the Bronx, with a metal gate on the window that blocked out the sky, his old home on St. Cruz seemed the most perfect place to be.

□3□

The train came to a sudden stop between stations. Marcus had no idea where he was or how long he'd been thinking about those first days in New York. The noisy children were gone and only a few passengers remained in the car. Maybe by studying the passengers he could figure out what train he was on and where it was going.

They looked like Brooklyn people—shopping bags, bundles, tired faces. So different from the American faces he used to see back home on St. Cruz. The tourist faces—pink and rich. The movie faces—pretty and happy . . . riding in long cars . . . owning gleaming homes and teeth. And the cowboys.

Who were these people in the train with him, with their tired black, white, brown, and yellow faces? They were Brooklyn people—not Americans. Maybe they were Bronx people.

Marcus tried not to stare but the faces were distracting . . . reminding him of things he didn't want to think about. The fear and loneliness of being in a strange place. The dream of America and the reality of New York City.

He had to concentrate on a plan. He couldn't stay in the subway forever. The train would eventually move and he'd have to go somewhere.

15

A woman in her twenties sat in the double seat near the door. She held onto a big package in the seat next to her. Something about her reminded him of Cassie. She was older than Cassie, but her velvety black skin and petite frame gnawed at his concentration, and he slipped once again into thoughts about those beginning school days.

□ 4 □

Marcus began his second day of school with more appre-
hension than the first. He knew what to expect now.
He started to walk to school, then changed his mind and
took the bus. The small, dark girl from his homeroom class
got on at the next stop. She had on the cleanest, starchiest
jeans he had ever seen. He wished he knew her name. She
looked straight ahead as she walked by him. He couldn't let
her get away.

"Hey, I, ah . . ." He touched her lightly on the arm. She
looked surprised at first and then gave him the same open
smile he remembered from the day before.

"Oh, hi."

"How you this morning?" He moved over and she sat next
to him.

"I'm fine. You okay?"

"Yes. What's your name?"

"Cassandra."

"That's a beautiful name."

"I hate it. Everybody calls me Sandra."

"I like Cassandra. It sounds like a song, you know. Can I
call you Cassandra?"

"Only if you whisper it." They both laughed. She reminded Marcus of his girl friend back home.

"What's your name?"

"Marcus."

"You like the school?"

"No. I sorry to say, I hate it."

"It's not so bad once you get used to it."

"It so different from back home."

"Where you from, Marcus? I like the way you talk. It sounds almost like you're singing."

"Then I go' sing your name, Cassandra. I from St. Cruz."

Marcus was surprised when she didn't leave him once they got off the bus. They walked to the school entrance together. She said hello to a few kids but stayed with him. Her friends looked curiously at her. She didn't seem to care.

When they reported to homeroom Marcus sat at a desk next to her. He hoped it wasn't anyone else's seat. Both he and Cassandra had the same homeroom and math class. When the first period bell rang most of the students left the room and a new group walked in.

Marcus's amber eyes sparkled playfully as he turned to Cassandra. For the moment he didn't mind being in school. "Cassandra, I go' call you Cassie. You like that name?"

She laughed. "Yeah, but don't call it out loud."

Mrs. Schwartz gave Marcus a mathematics test so she could determine his level. He wanted to tell her that shopkeepers never cheated him because he knew how to add, subtract, and multiply. He used to tell his friends in school, "What else you need to know? You go' fill up your head with some algebra and you ain't know when the people giving you wrong change."

Marcus watched the teacher's facial expression as she marked the test. Her eyebrows rose like two hairy mountains. She twisted her lips, shook her head, sighed, and walked over to him looking as if someone had just died. She

18

spoke very softly in funereal tones. "Marcus, you have to be put in a special mathematics class. Did you study math at all where you came from?"

He stared at her for a few seconds. "No, Miss. Me ain't study nutting a'tall. Me just play in de trees all day."

Cassandra tapped Marcus on the shoulder and said loudly, "In New York we play on the roof. Y'all really play in trees?"

The teacher turned to Cassandra. "Mind your business and get back to work."

He wanted to kiss Cassie for helping him anger the teacher. Cassie had a little smile around her mouth and he was trying hard to keep a straight face.

"Miss, I can count and make change and . . ."

The teacher said, "Marcus, that's not enough."

Cassie turned boldly to Marcus and the teacher. "She's gonna send you to that retarded math class."

"That's it, Sandra. I told you to mind your business!" Mrs. Schwartz said. "I am writing you up!"

The bell rang and Cassandra gathered up her books. "Cassie, I got you in trouble," Marcus said.

"No. Me and Schwartz always get into it. She ain't gonna do anything. She put me in that class when I first came here too, because I didn't pass that damn test she gives. I'll see you later, Marcus."

Marcus hoped she wouldn't get in trouble because of him, but he loved her spirit. Maybe things wouldn't be too bad. The social studies class was the same as the day before, except that the three big boys weren't there and the movie projector worked.

The teacher with the rusty voice still hadn't processed him for the class. Marcus looked at his program card to figure out what the course was. Economics I. It was still a mystery to him. Each time he changed classes he looked for Cassie. It was impossible to find that little face among the hundreds of students.

At lunchtime Marcus rushed to the cafeteria hoping to see her, but she wasn't there. He went outside without bothering to eat. Knots of students leaned against cars and stood in doorways. No one noticed Marcus, but he felt as if they were watching him without looking.

A part of him wanted to take the offensive and walk up to someone and slap the hell out of them. The tension would be relieved and the inevitable fight would be over with. A new boy always had to prove himself. He knew that. But there was only one of him and hundreds of them, so he walked away from the school.

He found a little concrete park with about five benches occupied by some elderly people. He sat on an empty bench and lit a cigarette. If he didn't want to see Cassandra so badly he wouldn't even bother to go back for the afternoon classes. There were so many students, who would miss him?

Marcus didn't see Cassie all afternoon. He rushed back to the homeroom class at three, but she had already left.

He looked for her the next morning when the bus got to her stop. She wasn't there. She rushed into homeroom just before the late bell rang. Before he could say anything to her, Mrs. Schwartz called him to her desk. "Marcus, you'll be taking mathematics in room 406." He snatched the piece of paper she handed him and walked quickly out of the room.

There were only ten students in the new mathematics class. The teacher gave him a sheet of simple addition exercises. The other students were oblivious to his presence. He finished in ten minutes and gave the teacher the paper. "Miss, I already know this." The teacher was helping a student who couldn't understand why seven multiplied by one did not

20

equal eight. Turning to Marcus she said, "Please, I'll be with you in a minute."

He went back to his seat and listened to her working with the other student. Now he understood what Cassandra had meant. He knew he didn't know a lot of math, but he also knew he didn't belong in that class.

The teacher came over to him with another sheet. This time it was subtraction of single digits. He stared at the paper for five minutes before doing the exercises, wondering whether the teacher was trying to make a fool out of him. He finished in fifteen minutes, but waited for another fifteen minutes before he went back to the teacher. "Miss, I know this already too."

"Young man, I wish I had a dollar for every student in this school who thinks he knows so much." The student she was working with looked up and said, "I guess she told you off, man."

Marcus placed the paper on the teacher's desk and walked out of the room. Luckily the bell rang by the time he reached the end of the hallway because he didn't know where he was going. He spent the rest of the morning listlessly waiting for lunchtime. Maybe he'd see Cassie then.

But he didn't see her for the rest of the day. He took a later bus the next morning and still no Cassie. As the bus pulled away from Cassie's stop it occurred to him that if he got to school after the first period he'd miss the mathematics class.

Marcus got off the bus near the Bronx Botanical Garden. This was the only spot in the Bronx that he liked. When he saw the tops of the evergreen trees he was reminded of his home in the islands. He walked along the clean street that ran parallel to the Garden. It amazed him that such an abundance of trees and foliage existed a few blocks away from the rubble and decay of tenements and vacant lots. He sat on a large stone outside the entrance gate and lit a cigarette. Even the air smelled fresher here. Marcus closed his eyes and made believe he was at the falls with Sellie and the Duncan brothers. After an hour or so had passed he went on to school.

On Friday he got off the bus by the Botanical Garden, sat on the rock, and smoked a cigarette. He imagined he was somewhere else, and congratulated himself on figuring out a way of avoiding his mathematics class. When he finished his third cigarette he walked slowly to school. He reached the building when the mathematics class was over. He sensed that something was going to happen. There were two fights that morning—one between two girls and another between a boy and a girl. He went from class to class like a zombie, all the time looking for Cassie. He skipped typing. Most of the typewriters were broken and he didn't want to share a machine with anyone else. Marcus went to study hall instead. He'd found out how easy it was to slip into the auditorium and act as if he belonged there. He opened his social studies text and pretended to read.

"You're studying hard."

He looked up. Cassie smiled at him. He quickly closed the book and tried not to show how happy he was to see her. "I just trying to catch up."

She laughed. "Catch up to what?"

The study hall teacher looked over at them. Marcus opened his book again. Cassie wrote something in her notebook. He wanted to sit next to her all weekend.

"Marcus, how you making out in that math class?"

He laughed. "I doing just fine. I took care of that problem."

22

She stared at him and he tried not to lower his eyelids. "What do you mean?"

"What I say. I took care of that problem."

Her eyes traveled over his face. "How?"

He liked the way she wouldn't let him go.

"In my own way."

"What way is that? You don't care if you in a retarded class?"

He crossed his eyes. "Maybe I belongs there."

"You're not retarded!" Her whole face seemed to smile.

"How you know?"

"I can tell by your eyes, Marcus. They're too bright."

"You a smart girl. You does read minds through eyes?"

"Got that right, Marcus. So be careful what you thinking when I'm around."

She rose quickly when the bell rang. "See you later, Marcus."

She left the room before he could say anything more. He thought about Sellie. If Sellie were there he'd say, Marcus, you too slow, boy. You still thinking up words in your head and the girl gone. Why you ain't ask her to meet you lunchtime?

Now that Cassandra was gone the tense feeling was back. Marcus went to his homeroom and got his jacket. As he ran down the stairs a girl said to him, "You big West Indian bastard." He slapped her hard in the mouth.

"Hey Eddie, that new boy slapped your woman," someone yelled. Marcus didn't go to the lunchroom. He walked out of the door and into the street. His long legs stretched out and he ran like some big graceful bird that can't fly. He didn't care where he was going, as long as it was far from the school. He ran so far that day, just as he ran now. That's

23

how he got to know the city. From running through it while running away from it.

When he got home he turned on the television. He stayed there until four o'clock, when his mother came in.

"Marcus, you fall asleep in front of the television again? Didn't I ask you to clear the dishes so I could start cooking when I came in?" Her face was strained and her movements tired.

"I forgot."

"You forgot? What else you have on your mind?"

"Mommy, I hate that school. I want to go back home."

"Marcus, I know it hard. But it won't always be so. It take time to get used to new things."

"I ain't go' never get used to it."

Marcus followed her into the kitchen as she talked.

"Marcus, I know you had a bad time. I know you miss your grannie and your friends. I miss home too. Lord, how I does miss my dear mother." Her voice trembled.

Marcus walked out of the kitchen. He knew he should stay and comfort her but he couldn't deal with her tears. He sat down in front of the television and she came into the living room wiping her eyes.

"Marcus, you really hurt me. You see I upset and you just rudely walk out the room. You think you the only one unhappy? I don't know what happen to you. You change so from the boy I left a year ago."

"Let's forget it. I ain't mean to upset you." He got up and put on his sweater.

"Where you going?"

"It stuffy in here."

It was a warm September evening. He went to the park and watched some young boys playing basketball. After an hour of that he walked aimlessly through Crotona Park and the surrounding crumbling streets. Marcus was in one of the biggest cities in the world and yet he felt as if he were in a tight little box. During his walk Marcus had decided not to go back to school for a while. He knew the boys wanted to fight him. Now one of them had a good excuse.

He returned home at eight o'clock, glad that both his parents had left for their night jobs. The living room also doubled as Marcus's bedroom. He opened up the couch, smoothed out the sheets and bedspread, and turned on the television. He lay across the bed and thought about the girl who had insulted him.

Someone had said, "Hey, Eddie, that new boy slapped your woman." He figured Eddie was one of the three boys from his social studies class. Maybe one of them had told the girl to say something. Marcus wasn't sorry he had slapped her. She deserved that. And he was satisfied with his decision to leave the school for a while. He needed time to get himself together. See what other things were possible for him. Look for some work. Maybe if he found a job his parents wouldn't worry so much about school.

□ 5 □

The train began to inch its way slowly, and for one hor-
rifying fraction of a second Marcus couldn't remember
why he was on the subway. He watched the small dark girl
gather up her shopping bag. The train picked up speed and
its motion brought him to full consciousness.

Why did things begin and end with Eddie? He should
have ignored him. Everyone knew Eddie was drunk. But he
couldn't let Eddie get away with that kind of talk. Not when
he was on the verge of straightening out his life . . . of understanding what was important . . . of learning what he
would have to do in order to get what he wanted.

It was Eddie who drew blood first. Marcus didn't want to
stab him. Didn't mean to kill him. He only wanted Eddie to
leave him alone. Eddie kept picking and picking. He asked
for it. Just like his girl friend asked to be slapped when she
called him a West Indian bastard.

The train eased into a station. Big, black graffiti letters
covered the windows and he couldn't tell which stop he was
at. When the doors opened, the girl with the shopping bag
walked out and Marcus followed her.

He glanced at the Grand Central Station sign as he was
caught up in the rush of people moving up the stairs. A po-

liceman stood at the top of the steps. Marcus saw him and moved in even closer with the crowd. He followed the largest group of people down a staircase without looking at the sign over it.

A shuttle train rolled into the station and Marcus rushed in with everyone else. The train sat there with its doors gaping open while Marcus tried to form a plan. However, neither the train nor Marcus's mind was moving forward.

□6□

Marcus left the house every morning as if he were going to school. He'd usually walk to his favorite spot by the Botanical Garden and pretend he was at the falls back in St. Cruz with Sellie and the Duncan brothers. When he was certain both of his parents had gone to work, he'd go home and spend the rest of the day watching television. Marcus didn't think about his situation. He waited, as if he were viewing someone else's life, to see what would happen next.

Ten days later his mother walked in from work waving a letter like a flag. At first Marcus didn't know what she was yelling about. "Boy, how you could do me this? I ask you just yesterday how you doing in school and you telling me fine. Your foot ain't touch the school steps in over a week."

Marcus got up quickly from the couch. He put his finger to his lips. "Mommy, please, I explain."

Her voice rose higher. "Explain? Explanation from a liar ain't nothing but a next big lie." Her voice sharpened like a blade and penetrated the bedroom door. His father crashed out of the room in his shorts and T-shirt. "What's this I hearing? You ain't in school? Louisa bring me a switch!"

Marcus saw his mother's anger turn to fear. She lowered her voice. "Rudy, wait. Talk to the boy. Ain't no tree switch, man. We in New York."

"Bring me a ironing cord. I cutting ass this night." Rudy pulled Marcus's shirt up to his chin. "You is a graduate now? Well I go' graduate your fresh tail right out this house after I put a diploma on your behind."

"Rudy, please. Talk to the boy. He too big for you to beat."

"He too big for me to beat? Then he too big for me to feed. He a big man? Then let him put a roof over his own stupid head."

"Rudy, man, please. He just need you to talk to him."

"Why you ain't talk to he? All I hear is you screaming. The boy need a good licking. He needed one for a long time."

Rudy loosened his hold on Marcus's shirt. Marcus stared at his father. "I ain't care about no education or no better life here. I can't get used to this place. I rather go to school back home."

Rudy slapped him across the mouth. His mother yelled. "Rudy, stop!" Rudy gripped Marcus's collar tightly. Marcus stared boldly at his father, unwilling to pretend that he was afraid.

"Boy, I and your mother make a lot of sacrifices to get all of we here. We kill we selves bringing you here, and you can't get used to things? As long as I paying you go' get used to whatever I say you have to get used to. Look like you got used to being illiterate." Marcus watched the veins in his father's temples strain at his skin as if they'd burst. Rudy pushed Marcus down on the couch and stormed back into the bedroom.

The event Marcus was waiting for had come, and now he knew what his next move would be. Somehow he'd have to leave his father's house and continue the journey he'd begun in St. Cruz.

His mother sat next to him on the couch. "Marcus, your father just tired. He work hard. Someday you understand.

29

At least you could get some kind of education here. Make some money. Maybe you go back home with something in your pockets. Marry a girl from home."

She put her arms around him and whispered softly. "Marcus, we don't have to stay here forever. Someday you could go back home and at least if you have money and education you could afford to send your children to school all year. Marcus, this was all me and your father could do for you. We bring you here. We ain't have nothing. All we could do is give you a chance to do something beside cut cane."

"Here is not what I expect. I thought I was coming to paradise. And daddy. We can't stay in the same house together."

"Don't say that. Your father loves you. I know he have a bad temper and he get excited. But he your father and someday you go' have children. Maybe then you understand. Now tell me why you ain't go to school."

He told his story quickly and dryly and then went to the closet and got his jacket. His mother walked over to him.

"Marcus, I know it's a hard adjustment, but please . . ."

"I don't want to talk again."

"Where you going?"

"For a walk."

Louisa must have told Rudy the story because the next morning when Marcus was leaving for school his father handed him a stick.

"Is you who go' have to deal with them boys. You go back to school and find the biggest, baddest boy there. Kick his behind good. Take this stick, you know how to stick fight. Butt some heads. You know how to butt head."

"Man, you going to get the boy hurt," Louisa said. "This ain't back home! This New York City!"

"All boys have to go through this thing. It like a ritual.

Marcus did plenty fighting back home. He no stranger to fights. The only thing some people understand is a good cut ass."

Louisa nervously washed a cup. She always found something to clean when she was upset.

"I don't like all this fighting," she said.

"Look, I tired. I don't like all this talking." Rudy stood directly in front of her. "All you enjoy making mountain out of molehill."

"You a fool, man. What good is a damn stick and everybody else have knife and gun?" Louisa asked.

Rudy turned to Marcus, who silently drank some tea. "He have to learn to fight his own battles. When you is black is a struggle from the womb to the tomb."

Louisa went over to the table and sat across from Marcus. "Marcus, can I trust you to take this note and yourself to school?"

"You been trusting him all the time. I go' make sure his shadow cross them school steps today."

Marcus looked up from his cup. "Daddy, I'll go to school."

"I know you going 'cause I taking you."

When they reached the school it seemed to Marcus that everyone was watching him and his father. He hoped Cassie wouldn't walk by now and see him being brought to school like a baby.

"I have a mind to go in and see them teachers, but I already late for work." Marcus stiffened as Rudy leaned into his face.

"I ain't carrying you to school like this again. Next time you take a holiday, I giving you a permanent vacation outside my house."

His mother had written a note stating that Marcus had been ill. He handed it to his homeroom teacher.

"I wondered what happened to you. Why didn't your parents contact the school?"

"They ain't know that's what they supposed to do."

"Well, one must inform people when one is not going to be where he or she is supposed to be, Marcus."

"Schwartz, get off Home Boy's back," said a boy standing in the doorway. "He don't know what the hell you talking about. One this and one that."

It was Ron, the boy from his social studies class. The students laughed and the teacher turned to the boy angrily. "Get out of here, Ron."

Ron ignored her. "I got a message for you, Home Boy— my friend Eddie wants to see you."

There was a smile in Ron's red-speckled eyes. Marcus wanted to smile, too. Ron had called him Home Boy, an expression he'd heard among the black boys when they greeted their friends. Being referred to that way made him feel like a part of the group—a member of the club.

Marcus walked away from the teacher's desk and headed for the doorway. He saw the look of surprise on Ron's face. "What Eddie want to see me for?"

"When you see him, he'll tell you." Ron turned around and walked down the hall.

Marcus was right. Eddie was one of the boys he had seen in the social studies class. He was sorry he'd left his father's stick home. If he had Sellie and the Duncan brothers with him the whole thing would be settled in five minutes.

Marcus took his seat near the back of the room. He'd give Eddie the fight he wanted. He wasn't planning on staying in the school too long, anyway. What difference did it make if he knocked a few heads together while he was here? Finding a job and getting away from his father took priority.

Marcus looked around the room for Cassandra. He wished she would come. Somehow everything seemed a little better when she was around. The bell rang, but Marcus remained in his seat. Some students stayed and others came into the class. Mrs. Schwartz was in the hallway talking to another teacher. Marcus figured he'd stay until she told him to leave. Since she seemed to think he was stupid, he'd act as if he didn't know where he belonged.

There were about forty students in the class. Everyone opened their notebooks and copied the math exercises from the blackboard. Marcus opened his notebook and copied them too. The board was filled with numbers in parentheses, small numbers next to larger digits—he copied them all.

The teacher came back in the room and began to mark a stack of papers. Everyone quietly worked on the problems. After Marcus finished copying the exercises, he peeped over at another student's paper. The boy had big, dirty erasure marks all over the page. A girl in front of Marcus scratched the part in her hair. The silence was broken by a loud "Damn!" from the other side of the room.

Mrs. Schwartz looked up. "Now, now. The problems aren't that difficult." She went back to her papers. Marcus wondered when she was going to teach. He half covered his paper with his arms, put his pencil in his mouth and stared at the numbers as if he were actually working on the problems.

Mrs. Schwartz stood up and went over to the blackboard. She called on a few students and together they worked out the answer for each exercise. Marcus sank down in his seat each time her eyes swept the room looking for a student to question. Finally the bell rang and Marcus relaxed.

He went to social studies expecting to see Eddie and the two other boys. Only Ron, the red-eyed boy, sat in the back of the room, reading the *Daily News*. Marcus liked the way Ron had sassed Mrs. Schwartz. It was too bad they were enemies. If a ball of paper bounced against his head during class, Marcus would get up and take care of Ron first. But the class ended without incident. Ron never looked up from his newspaper, and when the period ended he teased and played with a girl as he left the room.

Marcus spent the rest of the morning quietly thinking about Cassandra and St. Cruz and his pending fight. He didn't bother to go to the cafeteria at lunchtime. Instead he went outside and leaned against a car. A large group of boys came around the side of the school and Marcus braced himself. But Eddie and Ron weren't among them.

Marcus stayed there five minutes longer and then he began to feel foolish. It was a beautiful fall afternoon and here he was leaning against a car waiting for a fight. It occurred to him that the boys were just playing a stupid game—trying to scare him. Marcus decided to buy a candy bar and a pack of cigarettes and walk over to the Botanical Garden.

There was a greasy little candy store around the corner from the school. As soon as he entered he heard someone say, "That's him."

He looked around and saw Ron with Eddie and another boy. Other students from the school were also in the store. They all stared at him and Marcus stared back at them. Now that he and Eddie were face to face he wanted to run, but his pride was stronger than his fear. The boys walked over to him and the store owner yelled, "Y'all take that mess outside."

Marcus was amazed that the man knew what was about to happen. The three boys went outside. Marcus was still rooted to the spot where he stood. The man looked at him. "You too. Go!"

The boys stood in front of Marcus. Eddie looked at him sullenly, but Ron grinned as if he were participating in a big joke. "Hey, Home Boy, why you ain't been in school? You don't like us?"

Marcus realized that Ron was just clowning and agitating.

34

Eddie was the one who'd really fight him. Marcus decided to take care of Ron first. "If all you want to fight, then I go' fight each one alone."

Ron laughed. "You a funny-talking dude. You need to come to school so you can learn to talk, boy!"

Marcus saw Eddie moving closer. "You don't be slapping my woman and expect to get away with it," he said.

A group of students started to form. All three boys were almost evenly matched in height. Eddie was the tallest and Marcus was the thinnest. Without a word Marcus bent his head and rammed Ron in the chest. The speed and method of attack shocked Ron, and he was too slow to retaliate. Marcus saw Eddie moving in and gave him a hard kick in his groin. Then he tackled Ron and they both crashed into a plate-glass window. People yelled, and the store owner came out screaming and cursing in Spanish. Everyone ran.

Marcus headed up Fordham Road and caught a bus home. He didn't go inside immediately, but sat on his stoop and laughed. For the first time since he had come to New York he laughed from somewhere deep inside himself. He laughed like he did when it was carnival and they danced all day and night up and down the road. He laughed like the time he got the girl he was after without Sellie's lessons.

That evening his mother said, "Marcus, you seem like your old, happy self. You had a good day at school?"

"Yes. It the best day I have since I been here."

Ron was absent from school the next day. Eddie was there but he cut social studies; Marcus saw him later, playing basketball with some boys in the schoolyard.

At lunchtime Marcus finally ran into Cassandra. They ate together in the cafeteria. "I don't think Ron and them is going to bother you now," she said.

"You wasn't even here yesterday and you know more than me."

35

She smiled. "The whole school knows how you fought off them boys. They won't bother you anymore. Eddie can be nasty, though. He's always starting something."

"Whatever he start, I go finish." Marcus was his old self now. It was like being in St. Cruz and making his presence known among the tough city boys. "It's Ron I really messed up."

She grinned. "You sure did. He's a hard nut to crack, though. I heard all he got is one little knot upside his head and a scratch. Anyone else would've needed a hundred stitches with all that glass falling on them." Her expression turned serious. "Ron ain't so bad. He just goes too far sometimes. Especially when he's with Eddie."

Marcus leaned back in his chair and stared boldly at her.

"What's wrong?" she asked.

"Nothing. I just noticing how pretty you look. That red blouse does make me feel like a bull."

Marcus saw the little sparkle in her eyes and a shy smile forming on her lips.

"Well, I'm a good bullfighter, so watch it," she said. They laughed.

"Let's go out for a walk," he said. When they got outside several boys greeted him. A girl from his typing class smiled at him. Marcus was somewhere now.

He left for school on time the next day, hoping to meet Cassandra on the bus. When the bus reached her stop he had to force his face not to spread into a foolish grin when he saw her. She gave him a cool smile, but Marcus could tell by her eyes that she was happy to see him.

A small knot of boys stood at the corner of the school. Marcus didn't think anything of it until he noticed that Cassandra flinched slightly when she saw them. Then he spotted Eddie among them. He wondered whether Ron would be in

36

school. The boys didn't see Marcus, or if they did they didn't seem to notice him. Marcus thought no more about them. Now that they knew he wasn't afraid of them he expected no more trouble.

When the bell rang for the first period, Marcus remained in homeroom class. Cassandra nudged him. "Don't you belong in the other math class now?"

"I staying here."

"How? Schwartz will make you leave."

"No. Watch."

Cassandra laughed into her notebook all period, as Marcus seriously and slowly copied the problems from the board. A parent came to visit the teacher; one of the assistant principals came after the parent left; and the teacher only had a few remaining minutes to call on students and go over the problems.

After class he and Cassandra went out into the hallway and laughed. "See. I the invisible man," Marcus said.

"You are crazy, Marcus."

"Cassie, will you eat lunch with me again today?"

"Yeah, Marcus. See you at twelve."

During three o'clock homeroom Marcus was putting on his jacket when a boy came over to him and said, "Man, I hear Eddie's gonna get your West Indian a—"

Marcus was all over the boy before he finished his sentence. The other students moved chairs and desks to give the fighters room. Marcus beat the boy in his face. Everyone watched so quietly and intently that Mrs. Schwartz didn't know what was happening at first. When she discovered that they were fighting she shouted, "Break it up!"

Everyone ignored her. She looked pleadingly at the boys in the room. "Make them stop. Pull them apart!"

They still ignored her. When Marcus finished whipping

the boy, the other students put the desks and chairs back in place. The beaten boy left the room with a bloody nose. The teacher screamed hysterically at Marcus. "You're starting already? I thought you were a nice, quiet boy. I'm reporting this!"

Someone said, "Jamaica sure put a hurting on that boy." And from that day on everyone called him Jamaica.

Marcus sucked his teeth loudly at the teacher and sashayed out of the room with his new name. Cassie followed him.

They walked silently to the bus stop. When they sat down on the bus, Cassandra said, "You okay, Marcus?"

"I all right. You know I lose me temper. The boy make me so mad giving me some message from Eddie."

"When I saw Eddie and them boys this morning I figured something would happen again," Cassie said.

"I say it again. Whatever they start, I go' finish."

"Be careful, Marcus."

He knew the time was right and took her soft hands in his. He got off the bus with her and walked her to her building on 180th Street. The great ramshackle Bronx tenements no longer shocked him; yet the building didn't seem to be a place where Cassandra would live. She looked so clean and fresh and good as she flashed her even white teeth at him. He imagined her sitting on the veranda of one of those pink and white homes that the rich families owned back in St. Cruz. Somehow Cassandra had nothing to do with this background—a dirty, scarred stoop and a doorway hanging off its hinges.

□ 7 □

The screeching train jarred Marcus back to the present. He still leaned into the door. People rushed out of the car and a new group came in. Marcus left the train too, and saw that he was at Times Square.

Even though it was only one stop between Grand Central and Times Square, he felt as if he'd been riding for hours. What had happened to time? Times Square. That was the last place he wanted to be. He must have shuttled back and forth several times without realizing it. Maybe he should go out to the street. He could lose himself among the petty hustlers, pushers, thieves, and murderers out there on the strip. Maybe that's where he was supposed to be.

Marcus looked around for a clock. He wondered how many hours had passed since the fight. He had to call Cassie and let her know that he was okay.

He saw a sign pointing to the uptown train and decided to go to Harlem. He'd call Cassandra from up there and tell her to meet him somewhere in the area. She might even stay with him. She'd run away in the past, maybe she'd run away with him now. It would be easier to make a plan if Cassie were with him.

There were too many cops around Times Square. He'd

feel safer uptown. From the first day he came to New York and took a taxi ride through Harlem, he fell in love with it; after that he always referred to Harlem as his home away from home. He immediately recognized that if the tenements and lampposts were replaced with cottages and palm trees, Harlem could be St. Cruz. The faces were the same.

□ 8 □

Marcus's misery began even before he boarded the plane for the flight to New York City that afternoon in July. His mother had left alone a year before to begin building a new life for them in the United States. Now Marcus and his father would join her. Marcus was going to the States first because he was the eldest; the other children would be sent for later.

Marcus and his father hadn't spoken to one another since his grandmother died and Marcus had run away. The fight they had before she died created a chasm between him and his father that was impossible to close. As he fastened his seat belt, Marcus felt like a prisoner and his daddy seemed like the big, cruel jailer.

Marcus cried inside for the village, his dead grandmother, and the friends he thought he'd never be with again. Only the thought of seeing his mother after a year softened the edges of his hatred for his father. Marcus looked indifferently at the billowy cloud formations and the smiling stewardesses. It was his first plane ride but he could have been sitting on the back of a mule.

The size of Kennedy Airport jolted him back to life. Chrome and glass. Signs. Directions. Hundreds of people.

He'd never seen so many people at one time in one place. And everyone seemed to know where they were going but him.

He noticed that most of the people on the immigration line appeared nervous. His father looked worried and angry as he fingered some papers. A woman yelled at a whining child. Several people on the line stared at her and the baby as if the noisy little girl was going to get all of them in trouble.

Rudy handed a batch of papers to the officer and his voice was unusually soft as he answered the questions. But Marcus saw his father's balled fists and knew he was angry at having to respond to so many rudely asked questions. Marcus wished his father would make a mistake. Reply incorrectly so that the officer would send all of them back home. The officer stamped the papers and waved Marcus and Rudy away.

Marcus looked around for his mother, fearful that they'd never find her. She saw them first. "Oh God! Marcus, my baby! Look how tall you are. You grow like a weed." He buried his head in her soft neck. Her clean smell reminded him of home—their real home—St. Cruz. Rudy smiled slightly as he watched them embrace. Then Louisa and Rudy kissed each other. Marcus could now comfortably ignore his father.

Louisa's eyes were full of concern. Marcus knew she was aware of what had happened. He also knew she'd never talk about it unless she had to. She'd never say how hurt she was when she couldn't get to her mother's funeral or how frightened she'd been when she heard that Marcus had run away. For the first time since he was five years old he held her hands. "You go' get used to this place," she said. "It different from home, but we is better off."

She excitedly asked Rudy about their old friends in St. Cruz as they walked to the exit. Marcus was swept up in the crowd. "Hurry, Marcus." Louisa pushed him gently. He looked at her and saw how much she resembled his grandmother. There were unfamiliar lines in her face and new gray hairs. There was also something sad about everything she did, in spite of her animated conversation.

"Mommy, you happy here?" he asked.

"Of course, I happy. Now we is all almost together again. All is left is to get your sisters and brothers here."

Marcus stayed close beside her and Rudy while they pushed and shoved their way out of the airport and found a cab.

The tangled threads of roads, highways, and lanes confused him. There seemed to be thousands of cars. The excitement of it made him forget for a moment how unhappy he was. Marcus hardly knew where to look. He wished Sellie were there to see it all with him. Even Rudy seemed awed, looking first out of the rear windows and then out of the side windows.

The cab driver turned to his father. "There's some kind of tie-up. I think we'll make better time if we go through Manhattan, then into the Bronx. Okay with you?"

"I guess so, man. I ain't learn these highways yet."

Louisa was silent. The names of places they passed through were so unfamiliar to Marcus—except the Bronx. That's where his mother's letters came from. That's where his new home would be. Manhattan. He played around with the sounds. Man-hat-tan.

Once they left Queens there were no more trees or grass or anything green. At first Marcus didn't see the tenements or notice how big the buildings were. He only saw what

43

looked to him like hundreds of black people. He smiled and grabbed his mother's hand. "Mommy, this look like Princess Square during carnival, except nobody playing mas."

People stood in front of tables selling wigs, watches, shirts, perfume, jewelry, eight-track tapes, hats, lipstick, and a lot of other things he couldn't make out. He saw in their faces people he knew back home.

"Can we walk about some, Mommy?"

"Boy, you crazy?" Rudy yelled. "I tired from the trip. What I want to walk about a set of poor black people for? That's why I left St. Cruz." The cab driver, who was black also, smiled. Louisa said, "Marcus, this is Harlem. Don't set your foot on these streets. It bad here."

"Why it bad?"

"Don't question your mother," Rudy said. "If she say it bad, then it bad." Rudy looked at the cab driver. "What this avenue called?"

"West hundred twenty-fifth Street," the driver answered.

"It look like the marketplace back home, except here it ain't have no trees and it have such big, falling down buildings."

Marcus looked at the rows of buildings rising into the sky like concrete mountains. Rudy and the cab driver got into a long conversation about living in New York City. Louisa silently stared out of the window. Marcus wondered what she was thinking about. Marcus's amber eyes still held the island sunlight in them. Harlem fascinated him and he made a promise to return as soon as he learned his way around.

They left 125th Street and went over the Willis Avenue Bridge to the Bronx. When they got to the other side, Marcus thought his parents had taken him to hell. His eyes misted over.

The buildings were charred ruins. Windows looked like

black, empty eye sockets in a skull's head. Piles of brick and rubble stood like filthy monuments. "What's this? We ain't go' live here?"

"No," his mother said. "This is the South Bronx. People burn it out."

"Why?"

"Maybe they does like fires." His father laughed.

The cab driver looked at Marcus through the rearview mirror. "Landlords burn it out so people would move," the driver said.

"Why the hell all you bring me here!" Marcus cried. Tears stood on the edge of his thick, black lashes. His father's slap echoed through the small taxi.

"Who you criticizing?" Rudy asked. "You been here only a hour and this city already make you crazy? It been a long time since I give a lashing, but I ain't forget how."

Louisa looked embarrassed. The cab driver was trying not to laugh. Marcus's mother turned to him. "I know it seem terrible, but we could still do more here. Marcus, me and your father bring you here for a better life." She spoke soothingly.

Marcus watched two skinny dogs rooting in a mountain of bricks, bottles, wood, cans, rotten food, and dried dog feces. Rudy said, "See how big everything is here in this country? Ain't this the biggest pile of shit you ever saw?" Rudy and the driver roared with laughter. Louisa screamed. "Why you tease so? You know the boy upset."

"Upset? He ain't know what upset is," Rudy said. "Upset is spending the rest of your life in a dusty village. The harder you work, the hungrier you get. Those who ain't working is making all the money. That's upset. And it ain't go' change."

No one said anything. The driver nodded his head. Marcus saw little difference between the South Bronx and farther uptown on 179th Street where his mother lived. There were just as many burned-out buildings and boarded up stores. For the first time in his life he learned that blue skies and turquoise seas are not everywhere.

When they left the taxi the driver said to Rudy, "Watch your boy. These streets chewed up my son and spit him back out." He sped off before Rudy could respond.

The six-story building they entered looked like a prison or a hospital to Marcus. The light was broken in the hallway and the stench of urine choked him.

The tiny three-room apartment was shabby but spotlessly clean. Something about it reminded him of the small house they lived in back home. Suddenly he wanted to go back outside. In St. Cruz no one stayed crammed up in the house.

"How you like your new home?" Louisa asked. Her voice sounded as if she were afraid of the answer.

"It okay," Marcus said.

"It okay?" Rudy yelled. "That's all you could say? It okay?"

Louisa put her arms around Marcus and he felt her tremble slightly.

"I should have let you stay back home. Let you run wild with them ragged, dirty fools in the hills," Rudy said.

Louisa turned to Rudy. "I warning you, don't bring that up again. Leave the boy alone." Marcus saw that both of his parents looked tired. Their being here was all wrong. A mistake. He wondered if they realized that.

□9□

The train stopped at 96th Street and Marcus looked around again for a clock but didn't see one. The station was crowded, so he figured it must be past noon.

The train stopped at two more stations. A policeman entered the car at the second station and Marcus automatically jumped up and jammed his body between the closing doors. They opened again and he shot out—forgetting everything. He thought the policeman was chasing him.

He ran up the stairs and out into the street. The February wind pushed his body from behind. He didn't think about where he was. He ran. Had to get to Cassie and away from the policeman. He ran down 110th Street. He'd been down that street many times, but now it seemed as if he'd never seen the block before.

He found a narrow, stinking alley and stood against the wall. Even though it was cold, sweat poured from his forehead. He wiped his face with his jacket sleeve and struggled to compose himself. No one chased him. The policeman was probably still on the train, completely unaware of Marcus. Eddie probably wasn't even hurt and he, Marcus, was running all over the place like a fool. But the knife had gone in. He had felt it.

When he left the alley he recognized where he was. There was a small luncheonette on the corner. Marcus looked in and saw a telephone on the wall. The phone wasn't in a booth, so his conversation wouldn't be private. He'd just tell Cassandra to meet him in the luncheonette. His hands shook slightly as he dialed her number. The telephone rang three times. A husky, female voice answered.

"Can I talk to Cassandra?"

"She ain't here. Who is this?"

He hung up the telephone. Cassandra's aunt was the last person he wanted to talk to. The clock on the wall said two. It was too early. Cassandra wasn't home yet. Something had happened to his sense of time. It seemed as if he'd left school only an hour ago, but almost five hours had passed.

Marcus sat down at the counter and ordered a cup of coffee and a slice of pie. He didn't want the pie, but he didn't want the waiter to think he was a bum who could only afford a cup of coffee.

There were two other customers at the counter. Marcus relaxed. He sipped his coffee slowly and picked at the pie with his fork. A collection of postcards was pasted on the wall space between the coffee maker and the shelves of cigarettes. Stuck in the middle of the colorful postcards was a black-and-white poster of the New York skyline, dominated by the Empire State Building.

The poster reminded him of the postcards from New York that people sent to friends and relatives in St. Cruz. That's how he himself had expected New York to look. He stared at the poster and imagined the thousands of streets, avenues, and lives that skyline hid.

"Hey, man, you want some more coffee?" The man's gruff voice startled him.

"No. How much is this?"

48

Marcus paid the man and went back into the street. Then he remembered he wanted to call Cassandra. She wouldn't be home yet, though. He'd wait a while. Too bad he'd left the luncheonette. He hadn't even noticed the time when he walked out. He could have ordered another cup of coffee and remained a little longer.

It was getting cooler, but he didn't want to go back to the luncheonette. Ron. Maybe he could get to him. Ron must be worried too. They had become like brothers since that first fight. Crazy, red-eyed Ron. He remembered that there were telephones at the subway entrance. He'd call Ron, and then try Cassandra again.

A block before he reached the subway he saw a small tenement building. No one seemed to be going out or in. He wanted to wait a while before he tried Cassandra again, so he crossed the street and sat on the stoop. After he talked to Cassandra, he'd call Ron.

□10□

Marcus and Ron met in social studies class a week after the fight. They looked suspiciously at one another. Marcus felt himself to be in control now, especially when he saw the scar on Ron's forehead. Marcus had made his mark.

He walked to the back of the room and sat opposite Ron. Ron, as usual, read the *Daily News*. The two Spanish boys sat there bobbing their heads. These two is crazy, Marcus thought. Then he saw that they had plugs in their ears and cassette tape recorders. Marcus laughed. He took out his books and waited for the lesson. It never came.

The teacher was writing on the blackboard, "The War of 1812 . . ." when a student burst into the room. "Mrs. Jeffers, the principal says he wants these reports." She waved some papers in the teacher's face.

"Tell him I have a class now. I'll do them when the class is over." She went back to the board and continued writing. A few minutes later the same girl burst into the room again.

"The principal say you better get these reports to him now."

The teacher looked angry. Marcus turned to Ron. "Seem that the teacher can't teach," he said.

Ron rolled his eyes. "Man, I don't know why you sitting

there like Joe College. You learn more from this newspaper."

"Class, open your books to page one twenty-five. When I finish, we'll start the lesson."

"This just like the Old Goat, the professor back home," Marcus said. "All he tell you is to open book to such and such a page."

"I'm telling you, Jamaica, you best take half this *Daily News*. At least we can look at Ching Chow and figure out the number."

Marcus laughed. Even Ron knew his new name. The monitor stood in front of the teacher with her arms folded. Mrs. Jeffers said, "You can go back to the principal. I'll send the reports right away."

"No. He told me to wait."

Ron looked at the monitor. He laughed. "You take your job serious. How much they paying you, girl?"

"Mind your business."

"You two stop now," Mrs. Jeffers said.

"Tell him to mind his own business," the girl said again.

Marcus looked at his book. He turned to page 125. Suddenly there was a loud, whirring noise. One of the Spanish boys was rewinding his tape. Another teacher came into the room to ask Mrs. Jeffers how to do the reports. Ron said to the monitor, "Girl, you think you cute. Standing there looking like a baby moose." Everyone laughed.

The girl said, "Ron, you so damn ugly, nobody even want to be around you."

"Girl, you so ugly your shadow won't even follow you."

The class roared. The teacher began to look crazy. "Stop it, I say! Ron, I'll put you out. Young lady, you go back to the principal."

There was a loud blast of music. "We are fa-mi-ly, I got

all my sisters and me." Someone had pulled the ear plug out of the cassette recorder. The teacher ran over to the boy and tried to grab his recorder. Two girls began to dance. The bell rang. And the monitor stood with her arms folded, waiting for the reports.

Ron and Marcus reared back in their chairs laughing. "This a crazy class," Marcus said. "It fun, though."

"Going to all these classes is a waste of time," Ron said." I want me a job. Maybe I could learn something on a job."

Marcus picked up his books. Ron looked at him. "What class you have next?"

Marcus hesitated before he answered. "Economics."

"That's worse than this class. Come on outside for a smoke."

Marcus felt the tiny hairs on his arms rise. He thought Ron was trying to trick him. Get him outside the school and have several boys jump him. "Outside where? How you getting past the guards?"

"Don't worry. I got that under control." They walked out of the class together. Ron suddenly stopped in the middle of the hall and held his hands out. "Hey, man, I ain't trying to set you up. I figured you just like me, tired of this mess and want to go out for a smoke. I ain't the kind of dude who would pull something sneaky on a cat. That fight business is over."

Marcus liked the way Ron talked. He liked the sounds and the bouncy, familiar rhythms of the words. Ron reminded him of some of his friends back home. The kind of boy you could have for a partner. Someone to chase girls with, get in and out of trouble with, and someone you could depend on when you needed help.

They went down a staircase and Ron pulled out a pad with

the school name printed on it. "How you get the pad?" Marcus asked.

"Listen, that social studies teacher left it on her desk and I discovered it. You know, like Columbus discovered America?"

Ron leaned against the banister and started to write on the pad. "See, this is giving us permission to leave the building to run an errand for the teacher."

"What teacher? You does know how to forge handwriting?"

"Of course. I'll use one of those shop teachers. The female teachers write nice and neat. But I'll forge one of them old dudes in the shop. They write worse then me. Think I'll pick Sullivan. You know the one in the wood shop? I'll say we going to pick up supplies. Sullivan be easy to forge. He can't even spell."

Marcus laughed. Ron had a mischievous smile as he composed the note. When Ron finished they left the staircase and walked quickly down the hall. Marcus fell in with Ron's stride. Marcus liked the smooth, swaying walk of the black boys. It was the kind of walk Sellie was always imitating, but never got right. Marcus didn't have the talk yet, but he had the walk. He had that back home. He had learned it from a boy named Rufus who went to New York and came back to the island with a New York style.

"Suppose the guards check with the teacher before they let us go?"

"You smart, Jamaica. But I got that covered too. We going to Blake. He lazy and ain't going to check nothing. He be glad if everybody in here walked out so he wouldn't have nothing to do."

Ron walked over to Blake, who was reading a newspaper.

"Hey, man, ain't you supposed to be patrolling these halls. How you gonna keep this school safe?"

Blake put down his paper and stared at Ron. "Who died and left you in charge?"

"Must be you. The way you sit in one spot all day you can't be alive."

Marcus stifled a laugh. He loved the way Ron agitated the guard. Blake made a tired motion as if he were going to stand up.

"What you guys want?"

"We got to go out for Sullivan."

"You have a note?"

"Yeah. Want to see it?"

"Of course I want to see it. Why you think I asked?" Blake stood up. He and Ron were the same height.

Ron laughed. "Sure you can read, Blake?"

Blake's jaws worked back and forth as he snatched the note from Ron. "Boy, you like a pair of tight shoes. A damn pain. Get out of here!"

They walked around the corner from the school and sat on a bench in the small concrete park. Ron pulled out a pack of cigarettes and offered Marcus one. "Where you learn that crazy jungle fighting?"

Marcus laughed. "Is how we fight back home. We stick fight and we ram our heads like goats."

Ron drew heavily on his cigarette. "You know, when I was down home them country boys be doing some crazy fighting like that."

"You ain't from New York?"

"Naw. Come from down south. Came here two years ago."

"You like New York?"

"It's all right, I guess. But people in New York is wild."

Marcus was surprised. He thought Ron was wild. "You was frighten when you first came from down south?"

"Yeah, man. I never saw so many different kinds of people before. Down home people just be black or white."

"Yes. I ain't never see a place like this either. When I landed at the airport I just wanted to turn around and go back home."

"You miss your home?" Ron looked at Marcus closely.

"Yes, man. I wishing every day I could go back."

"Sometimes I be thinking about how we used to go way out to the country in the summer," Ron said. "People out there be poor, but they don't live like people in New York. I mean, the way people be living in these big, dirty buildings. My uncle had a little farm. We played in the fields. Went swimming in the creek. Ran after girls in the bushes. My aunt and uncle's house was old, but it was clean on the inside. There was a time when we didn't even have a toilet in the house."

Marcus tried to look above the buildings and bring only the blue sky into his field of vision. "I guess we was poor too. I used to live in the village with my grandmother. We ain't have no toilet in the house, neither. My best friend, Sellie, show me how to swim, smoke cigarette, and catch girl in the high grass. My grandmother keep her house just so. Like you say, it ain't look pretty from outside, but it was clean, clean inside." Marcus took a long drag on his cigarette and watched the smoke curl up to the sky. "So you a home boy too, Ron. You from somewhere else."

"Most people in New York is from somewhere else. New York ain't never felt like no real home to me, Jamaica."

Marcus crushed his cigarette with his foot. "I know how you feel."

Marcus and Ron went back to school in time for their next class. He was glad they had cut economics. Marcus still couldn't get past the teacher's rusty voice and thick glasses. Maybe he'd go to the class tomorrow. For today, it was more important that he accept Ron's offer of friendship; neither one of them wanted to fight the other again.

Cassandra seemed to be waiting for Marcus outside their homeroom class at lunchtime, but he wasn't sure. They went to the cafeteria together. As they took trays and stood on line, a few more students said hello to him. "It look like I fight the right people. I popular now."

Cassandra smiled. "That's the only thing some of these fools around here understand. You got over this time, Marcus. But be careful. Some of these people fight dirty, if you know what I mean."

"I know. Look, I ain't bothering nobody unless they bother me." He watched her daintily cut the meatballs on her plate. "You don't keep a lot of friends in school, do you?" he asked.

"Nope. A lot of friends mean a lot of trouble."

"I had fun with my friends back home."

"Maybe things is different where you come from. Your friends don't get you in trouble."

He laughed, thinking about all of the scraps he and Sellie and the Duncan brothers got into. "You should have friends, Cassie."

"I do, but not here at school. There's people I talk to here, but no real good friends."

"You have a boyfriend?"

"No one special."

"What that mean?"

Her eyes gave her away. "Cassie, I see a devilish look in your face. You teasing me."

56

She looked down at her plate and laughed. She seemed embarrassed and not so sophisticated now, which made Marcus feel so secure that he dropped the conversation. When they finished eating, they went outside.

It was a red and gold Indian summer day so they walked to the concrete park. As they passed the schoolyard, Ron, Eddie, and some other boys were playing basketball. Ron yelled, "Yo, Jamaica." Marcus waved. He saw Eddie say something to the other boys. He could tell by the way they laughed that he had said something rude. Ron kept throwing the ball in the basket as if he hadn't heard.

Cassandra frowned. "See Marcus, that Eddie always got something smart to say."

"I don't look for problem. But he messing with the wrong person." They sat down on an empty bench in the park. A few old men were on another bench playing checkers.

Marcus eased his arm across the back of the bench, and let his hand dangle over the edge. Then he slowly moved his arm until he touched Cassandra's shoulder lightly. She didn't move, so he let his arm rest across her shoulder and she sort of nestled into its curve. He wanted to stay there for the rest of the day. He could tell by the comfortable look on her face that she felt as good as he did. The feeling lasted for the rest of the afternoon at school.

At three o'clock they left the building together and Cassie suggested that they walk home. The October afternoon was still warm. "You like to walk, Cassie? Most people here don't walk much."

"It's nice out and I don't feel like being with all of them wild people on the bus."

Initially he thought she wanted to spend more time with him. As they walked quickly up Fordham Road he sensed

57

that something was bothering her. "What's wrong, Cassie?"

"Nothing. It's just school. I had a bad afternoon. I'm mad. I feel like walking my madness off."

"You running like someone chasing you."

"I want to get away from here as fast as possible."

When they neared the Botanical Garden Marcus impulsively said, "Cassie, come walk with me over there by the Garden."

"Okay, Marcus."

He was surprised that she agreed so quickly, since she was in such a hurry before. He took her to his favorite spot.

"It remind me of home. You don't see big buildings here. Just all the trees," he said.

"I never noticed how pretty it is over here. It's like when I was real little and I went to South Carolina with my aunt and uncle. We were in the country and it was so pretty."

"I go' take you back home with me one day, Cassie."

"Stop jiving, Marcus."

"I serious." He took her in his arms and kissed her. Their bodies fit like two matching pieces of a puzzle. She rested her head on his shoulders. "You not vexed anymore?" he asked.

"Vexed? What's that. Oh, you mean mad."

"Back home, mad mean someone crazy. You not crazy."

"Well, we say mad to mean angry. I guess you can be so angry it drives you mad."

He weaved his rough, calloused fingers through hers. "Cassie, tell me why you was angry today."

"Eddie and some other boys were going to gang up on you at the bus stop."

He let her hand go. "Why you ain't tell me? That why you have me walking all over the road. You should tell me."

"Marcus, how you going to fight ten boys?"

58

"I going to have to fight Eddie. My father's right. Is the only thing some people understand—a good cut ass."

"You already had two fights."

"Things come in threes. I going to have the third fight with Mr. Eddie."

"Forget it. By tomorrow that fool's mind be on something else."

"I go' have to fight. And you should tell me. I would go right to the bus stop and talk to the boy with my hands."

"You're feeling like a boxer now. That's why Ron told me not to tell you anything until we were away from the school."

"Ron? He know? He with them too?"

"No. He told me to warn you. Just stay out of Eddie's way for a while. He'll forget about it and go on to bother someone else."

"Too bad I ain't mush him up good when I had the chance."

"Be careful, Marcus." She looked at her watch. "I gotta get home."

"You must be home at a certain time?"

"Yeah. I baby-sit for this lady in my building."

Marcus suddenly felt useless. Everyone seemed to have something to do but him. He walked Cassandra down Crotona Avenue to her building on 180th Street. He didn't want to leave her. He kissed her good-bye and promised to meet her the next morning. As he walked home he wondered how he could be so happy all day and suddenly feel so rotten.

By the time he reached his house he felt again that he wasn't a part of his surroundings. It was still too early for his mother to be home and his father hadn't arrived yet. He turned on the television, but it didn't help him. The frenetic image of Lucille Ball only removed him even further from his surroundings. He didn't want to fight anymore; he didn't even want to cut classes. If he could get a job, make some money, and understand in which direction he was moving, maybe he'd be able to feel good about something for more than three hours.

Marcus turned off the television and went to his parents' bedroom. Though he didn't want to fight again, the first issue Marcus decided to handle was Eddie. He searched for the stick his father had offered him the other day. The stick wasn't there, but he found a short, fat club that could be tucked inside his looseleaf notebook.

When he met Cassandra the next morning his mood was still heavy. But his heart raced a little when he saw her standing on her stoop. She wore a pleated skirt and black tights. It was the first time he'd seen her without those clean, starched jeans. She had the kind of plump, round legs he liked.

"Let's walk so I can show off this pretty girl I have." He took her hand.

She leaned into his arm. "We can walk home this afternoon."

"Why you love to walk home so?"

"After you been hassled all day you need to walk."

"Maybe you think it dangerous to ride?"

"You talking about Eddie?"

"Yes. But I have something for him today. It go' fit right on top his head."

"Marcus, leave it alone, please."

"I can't let him threaten me and get away with it."

"Why don't you try to get yourself together. They gonna eventually find out you been cutting that math class."

"I can't do school lessons until I give Eddie some instruction."

"You make me laugh, Marcus. The way you say things. But I'm serious."

"I serious too."

They climbed on the bus and he put his arms around her when they were seated. She stared out the window and a little mischievous smile came across his face. "Hey Cassie, let me come by your house so you could help me with me studies."

He expected her to laugh, but the question seemed to disturb her. Before she could respond he said, "Doesn't your mother and father let boys visit you?"

"My mother is dead and I don't have a father."

"Cassie, how you mean? Your mother make you alone?"

"You know what I mean."

"Everyone have a father."

"I don't know who my father is."

"No one ever tell you who he is or was?" Marcus shook his head. "I never hear of something like that. Back home everyone know his father. He could be a lot of other people father too, but you know who he is."

"My aunt told me once that he was no good. After that I didn't care who or where he was."

She was getting more agitated, so Marcus dropped the questions about her father. "Will your aunt let you have company?"

"Yes, but . . . well, Marcus, my house ain't so fancy, and sometimes my aunt can be—"

"Cassie, I ain't coming to look after your house or your aunt. I coming to see you and where I live ain't no palace either."

When they got off the bus Marcus looked around but he didn't see Eddie. It didn't matter. Whenever he saw him

61

he'd be ready. He and Cassandra went to homeroom class. When the bell rang for the first period classes, he decided to take a chance and stay there. But the teacher looked at him as if she were beginning to remember that he didn't belong in the class.

"Cassie, I going to that dumb math class," he said.

"Yeah, Marcus. Schwartz is looking at you in a funny way. I'll meet you for lunch."

As Marcus walked down the crowded hall he made certain that the club was still in his notebook.

"Hey, Jamaica." It was Ron.

Marcus didn't smile. "I hear your friend was stalking me yesterday."

"Yeah. Don't pay him no mind. Eddie crazy, man."

"I ain't 'fraid him, you know."

"I know. And he know it too. Look, I tried to talk to the guy. I don't know what's wrong with him, man."

"You and he is friends, yes?"

"We ain't real tight. I talk to him in school—for the laughs, you know. He acts too crazy sometimes."

Marcus stopped in front of the door to his math class. Ron said, "Come on with me. I got a real pass from Sullivan to go and get some supplies from the hardware store."

Marcus looked in the room. The ten students in the class were hunched over their papers, working intently, while the teacher showed a boy how to count change with play money.

"I'll go with you," Marcus said.

After Ron purchased the supplies, he and Marcus stopped by the small park near the school. "You know how to play basketball, Jamaica?"

"No, but I like the game."

"What y'all play where you come from?"

"Soccer most of the time."

"Want to learn how to play basketball?"

"Yes. I always watch the boys in gym."

"Come around my block after school and we'll shoot some baskets.

"Okay."

Marcus met Cassandra at lunchtime. While he ate he realized that his bad mood had passed. They walked over to the small park after they'd eaten. Eddie was nowhere in sight.

After school, he and Cassandra walked slowly up Fordham Road, both enjoying the brisk autumn air. "I didn't see Eddie in school today," she said. "I told you he was just a fool."

"I go' show him how a fool feel if he keep harassing me."

"Forget him. How you make out in the math class?"

Marcus dreaded the question. "I make out okay."

"You need to see Mrs. Jones, the guidance counselor. She'll take you out of that class."

"I go see her tomorrow."

After he walked Cassandra to her house, he went home and dropped off his books. Ron waited for him at the playground. He showed Marcus various shots and told him the rules of the game.

They played one on one. Marcus made hook shots, dunked the ball a few times, and dribbled the way he had seen the boys do it at school. He was well coordinated and learned quickly.

Ron said, "You sure you ain't hustling me, Marcus? You never played before?"

"No, man. I swear. I just watching all the time."

"Come over here tomorrow. Some of my boys be here and you can play with us."

Marcus was hungry, tired, and happy when he got home. Rudy was leaving for work as Marcus put the key in the door.

"Which place you was?"

"Daddy, I was playing ball with a friend."

"What friend?"

"A boy from school."

"You be careful. I ain't bring you here to run like a wild stallion. Your mother was worried."

"Daddy, this the first time I ever go somewhere from school. All you act like I been missing for two days."

"Give me your lip one more time and I go' play ball with it."

Rudy slammed the door, and walked quickly down the stairs. Louisa had already gone to her night job, but she had left Marcus's food on the stove. It was strange sitting there in the kitchen eating alone, but in a way he liked it. He didn't have his father's heavy presence or his mother's nervous looks and questions to deal with. He took his plate into the living room and turned on the television.

The next morning he met Cassandra. They rode the bus to school. Marcus still had his club. Eddie would return to school sometime, and Marcus would be ready for him.

The bell for his first period class rang, and Marcus, at first planning to remain where he was, decided to try once more to do the correct thing. "Cassie, what room the guidance counselor in? I going to straighten out this math business."

He hurried down the packed hall to the exit. When he got downstairs to the first floor, it was crowded with latecomers still milling around. A girl's loud laughter attracted his attention. He looked around and saw the same girl he'd slapped a few weeks ago—Eddie's girl friend.

Eddie stood a few feet away from her talking to some boys. There were two guards posted at the front entrance. This would be a stupid place to start a fight, Marcus thought. He walked over to the group of boys. Eddie's girl friend looked at Marcus as if he were the strangest thing she ever saw.

"Eddie, I hear you looking for me," Marcus said. "I'll see you for lunch. I have a big, fat knuckle sandwich for you."

Everyone laughed. One of the boys said, "Eddie I wouldn't take that if I was you."

"I got something for you, little banana boy," Eddie sneered. "And you getting it right now."

As Eddie rushed at him, Marcus pulled out his club and dropped his notebook. He hit Eddie on the side of his forehead.

Someone restrained him. "Hey, Jamaica, man. Don't do this. You get in serious trouble." It was Ron who held his wrists.

A guard held Eddie, who kept yelling. "I'm gonna tear you up. I'm gonna get your West Indian . . ."

"Ron, let me go," Marcus said. "I got to close that hole he have for a mouth."

"Ron, what you doing? Let him go. Who you supposed to be, the law?" Eddie yelled.

A large crowd had gathered. One guard tried to get everyone back to class and another attempted to talk to Eddie, but his voice couldn't be heard above the shouting.

Ron kept talking. "Jamaica, the dude ain't worth you getting thrown out of school over."

The veins in Marcus's temples stood out. His eyes were fixed on Eddie. With a thrust of force he broke away from Ron and was all over Eddie again. Ron and two other guards from the opposite side of the hall jumped into the fray.

Teachers rushed out of their rooms. Ron, Eddie, Marcus, and a guard were on the floor. Another guard and two boys tried to pull the jumbled mass apart. The two original guards tried unsuccessfully to clear the hall. An assistant principal came out of his office screaming. He wore a toupee, and one

65

of the girls said, "Careful, Mr. Michaels, you'll flip your wig."

"What is this? Guards! Break them up," Mr. Michaels said.

"What you think they doing?" a boy said.

The boys were finally separated. Marcus's shirt was torn. Eddie had a bruise under his eye and a knot on the side of his forehead. Ron had a cut over his lip. The assistant principal yelled. "I am outraged! You three boys into my office!"

Someone gave Ron a tissue for his lip. Two of the guards went into the office with the boys. The assistant principal's face was red and his toupee looked as if it were going to fall off. Mr. Michaels took their names and homeroom numbers. Marcus stared out of the window, not even looking at the assistant principal as he answered his questions.

Mr. Michaels said, "I'm suspending all three of you until you come back with your parents. You cannot return to school without your parents."

Ron said, "Mr. Michaels, I was . . ."

One of the guards interrupted. "Ron was breaking up the fight."

"That's why we have guards. As far as I'm concerned he was in the fight too."

Marcus turned to Mr. Michaels for the first time since he came into the room. "He was trying to keep me from fighting. He ain't in this thing at all."

"Well, I guess you got your friend in trouble. He's suspended too. I'll have the secretary type the letter for your parents."

After Mr. Michaels gave them their letters, he told them to go back to their classes. As they left the office, a student came over to Marcus and handed him his notebook. The club was back inside. The boy said, "Wanted to make sure you got your stuff back."

"Thanks, man," Marcus said.

Eddie looked at Marcus. "This ain't finished yet."

Ron said, "Man, why don't you ice it."

Marcus laughed. "It all right. He like whippings and I go' give him what he like."

"You guys cut it out," a guard said. "Y'all in enough trouble already."

Eddie ran up the staircase still mumbling to himself. Ron turned to Marcus as the guard went up the stairs behind Eddie. "I ain't staying in here the rest of the day if I'm suspended. I'm leaving now," Ron said.

"I too. My father go' bellow like a wounded bull when he hear 'bout this."

They walked over to the young guard, Blake, posted at the main entrance. He let them leave the building when they showed him their letters. They went to Ron's house.

Marcus was surprised to see that Ron's building was in worse condition than his. A recent fire had practically gutted the hallway.

Ron's apartment was the real surprise. Delicate flowered curtains hung at the windows. Lush, green plants were on the sills and on stands. Family portraits and colorful pictures covered the walls. The two mahogany end tables had a brilliant shine, and crocheted pillows decorated the big comfortable-looking couch. A cane-seated mahogany rocker was placed before the television set. An imitation oriental rug covered the spotless floor.

"Sit down, man. Make yourself at home."

"This a beautiful place, Ron."

"Thanks. My moms say you could live in a cave and still keep it clean."

"Me grandmother used to say the same thing."

67

Ron brought some sodas and potato chips into the living room. "My mom's gonna be mad about this mess. But I keep telling her I want to quit school. I hate that place."

"You want to go to another school?"

"No. I want a job. I'm sick of school. Ain't learned nothing in no school since the sixth grade. My father is dead and my moms works. She need some help, but she want me to stay in school."

Marcus took a long gulp of soda. "My father say it have educational opportunity here that it don't have no place else."

"Oh yeah? No one ever told me about them. I want a job."

"People say you have to have a good education to make money," Marcus said.

"Maybe for some jobs. I like to do things. Make things. I ain't for sitting in no schoolroom all day long. That ain't me."

Marcus nodded his head. "I not big on school either. Back home I go to school for five months and cut cane for five months. All of we children work during cane season to help the family. My father say is a lot of money here in this country. That's what I want too—a good job."

"How much money you make in them sugar cane fields?"

"About three dollars a day. It's according to how much cane you cut."

"That's all? Negroes be doing bad all over the world. I mean, that's about all we used to make down home in the summer when we kids go in them fields and pick beans for one of the farmers."

Marcus looked at a framed photograph on a table of three young girls in white dresses with large bows in their hair. The picture reminded him of his sisters. He tried to imitate Ron's accent. "Negroes be looking alike all over the world too!"

68

Ron laughed. "You got that right, Home Boy."

When they'd finished their sodas, they met Ron's friends in the playground. Marcus played ball with the boys and after the game one of Ron's friends said, "That boy ain't no scrub. He play pretty good ball for a foreigner."

Marcus felt so good that even the suspension from school didn't worry him. Soon he'd be beating those boys at their own game. As he walked home, he thought about what would happen when he told his parents about the suspension. His father would yell and threaten. Then his mother would plead with his father, she'd start to cry, and the whole thing would be over. Though he felt strong and confident, he decided not to show Rudy the letter from school until his mother was there. He didn't have the nerve to face Rudy's anger by himself.

When Marcus reached home Rudy had already left for work. Marcus took a long, hot shower and let the water soothe his sore body. The only thing he regretted about the day was not walking Cassandra home. He'd get her telephone number tomorrow. He knew his parents would have him back in school the next day, because they were so determined that that was where he belonged.

□11□

Judging by the growing traffic and the cooler air, Marcus guessed it was nearing 3:30. He shivered. The light jacket he wore wasn't warm enough for the oncoming February evening. Once again, he tried to organize himself. Maybe he'd call Ron first and then Cassie.

Marcus left the stoop where he'd been sitting and walked across the street to the three telephones at the subway entrance. The first telephone didn't work, but he got his dime back. He tried the other two and they didn't work either. He lost his dime in the last one. There wasn't another telephone booth in sight, and most likely if there was one it wouldn't be working either.

The luncheonette had the only guaranteed telephone, but he didn't want to go back there. He thought the men had looked at him in a suspicious way. He had three quarters and a five-dollar bill. All of his small change was gone. He walked reluctantly back to the luncheonette. He'd make his two calls and leave. There was a different man behind the counter and no other customers.

"Can I have change for the phone?"

The man cleared off the counter. "We don't usually give change if you ain't buying."

"Give me a cup of coffee."

Even though the man stared at him, Marcus saw something kind and generous in his face. "Forget it, son, here's the change."

Marcus practically held his breath as the telephone rang.

"Hello." It was Ron's mother.

"Is Ron there?"

"No. Is that you Marcus?" She sounded excited, as if she were expecting his call.

He slammed the telephone in her ear and was immediately sorry. From the way she had yelled into the phone he was certain she knew what had happened. She'd try to convince him to give himself up to the police, then she'd start praying for him. He loved Ron's mother almost as much as he loved his own, but he couldn't talk to her now. He lowered his head and leaned against the wall.

The counterman said, "Here son, have some coffee on the house."

Marcus's shaking hands spilled some of the liquid when he picked up the cup.

The man stared at him again as he wiped the counter. "Winter ain't gone yet. It's cold out there."

Marcus spoke into the cup. "Yes. It cold."

"You're from the Caribbean?"

"Yes."

"Where?"

"St. Cruz."

"Oh yes. I know it. I was there once when I was in the Merchant Marines. The capital, Sabia, is a beautiful little town. The whole island is beautiful."

Marcus looked up. It was the first time that he'd met someone who knew about a Caribbean island other than Jamaica.

"Yes. It a beautiful place."

"I know you may still have all of that island heat in your blood, but you shouldn't be out at night with only a jacket."

"I don't like winter."

"Who does? Winter ain't a normal time. It's a dead time. Come in this place in the summer and it's packed."

"When was you in St. Cruz?"

"Long time ago. In the sixties, before I bought this business. You miss your home, don't you, boy? Someday you may go back—if you keep yourself out of trouble and don't put your mind in jail. It's a big world out there, son."

The man detected Marcus's hands tightening around the cup. "I didn't mean go to jail," he said. "I mean, don't lock up your mind. Stretch out. This ain't all there is."

Marcus swallowed the last of the coffee.

"Want some more?" the man asked. Marcus nodded. The man gave him another cup and then went to take care of a customer who had just walked in.

Marcus took a sip of the coffee and decided to call Ron again. He'd talk to Ron's mother if he still wasn't in. He dialed the first three digits and hung up. He needed Ron or Cassandra. He didn't want to talk to anyone's mother or father—not even his own.

Two young women came into the luncheonette and gave the owner a big hello. It was like a family place. Everyone seemed to know the owner and any other customer who might be in there. He, Marcus, was the only unknown element, and he figured he'd better keep it that way.

Marcus didn't want to go back out in the cold, but the restaurant was too bright and open. Too many people were strolling in. He needed to be alone to plan. But he still needed to speak to Cassie and tell her to meet him in the restaurant. She'd help him. Stay with him. They'd work things out together.

He went back to the telephone and dialed Cassandra's number. The line was busy. He couldn't stay there any longer. He'd meet Cassie someplace else.

"How much I owe you?" he asked the man.

"Nothing son. Like I said, it's on the house."

Marcus thanked the man, left the luncheonette and started toward the subway without thinking about why he was heading in that direction. It was getting very cold now. He needed to find a warm, dark place. Instead of continuing across 110th Street, he walked downtown, not even realizing what street he was on.

When he came to a movie theater he took out the five-dollar bill and bought a ticket without actually noting what movie was playing. He sat way up in the balcony. The movie had just begun. It was an old kung fu movie. When he saw the images kicking and flying on the screen he thought of the first time he'd gone to a Bruce Lee movie with Ron.

□ 12 □

They were so happy because they'd made twenty dollars apiece helping out in a grocery store on Ron's block. They had fetched and stacked numerous cans, tins, boxes, and crates from ten in the morning until seven in the evening on Saturday. Sunday they went to the Bruce Lee movie.

This was a few days after the suspension from school. Before he went to bed that night, Marcus had left the letter on the kitchen table so that his mother or father would see it when they came in. He hoped his mother would see it first, but was resigned to the fact that his father would find out eventually.

Louisa's yelling woke him up. He figured that Rudy wasn't there because she had more control when he was around. Marcus didn't listen to anything she said. When she finished he replied, "But Mommy, I only do what Daddy say. He tell me to fight back so no one bother me."

"You and your father both such big, smart men. But is me who have to put you back together when one of them hooligans tear you apart."

The next morning Marcus geared himself for his father's yelling and screaming. He washed up and made coffee.

74

Louisa came into the kitchen fully dressed. "Hurry, Marcus. I going to that school with you, then I have to get to work." She spoke softly so that his father wouldn't hear.

Louisa was so angry that Marcus didn't say anything—not even to thank her for not telling Rudy. He would have liked to hug her but knew she was like a hot, smoldering coal. They rode silently to school. Louisa met all of his teachers and promised them that Marcus would do better.

When they left the assistant principal's office, Ron was coming in with his mother. Marcus wanted to laugh. Ron looked as solemn as a preacher. His tall, lean frame slouched slightly and the cap he usually wore turned backward was held repentantly in his hands.

Ron kept a straight, serious face when he saw Marcus. "Hello, Marcus, I want you to meet my mother-dear."

Ron's mother was tall and imposing. She rolled her eyes at Ron as if she wanted to knock him from one end of the hallway to the other. Marcus and Louisa both said hello to her. Marcus laughed when Ron winked as he followed his mother into the office.

Louisa frowned. "Is that the boy who been teaching you how to stay in trouble?"

"Is my friend, Ron. It was he who try and help me."

"These black people here don't take care of their children properly," his mother said. "You never did know how to pick decent friends. Even back home, that lazy Sellie and them rank Dudley brothers."

Marcus looked up at the ceiling. Why did she have to go all the way back home and talk about his friends there?

"The next time something happen with you in this school I telling your father. And I don't like that boy. So black with such a red eye." Marcus wanted to laugh but kept his head bowed respectfully.

"Hey, Home Boy, they thought they got rid of us, but we back again," Ron yelled at Marcus across the social studies class. Ron had returned to the class first.

Marcus strutted to the back of the room and sat opposite him. "I wish they throw me out for good."

Ron closed his *Daily News.* "Michaels told my moms the next time I get in trouble they gonna suspend me permanently. She got upset. But it was like Michaels enjoyed upsetting her."

Marcus leaned back in his chair. "He told my mother that I was falling in with a bad crowd. He said he knew I was a good boy because most of the students who came from the islands was different. We behave better than American students."

"He always do that," Ron said. "Just trying to turn your mother against me."

The teacher looked over at them and Ron opened his newspaper and started reading it as if it were a textbook. When the teacher went to the blackboard again, Marcus leaned over to Ron and whispered, "Wonder what he told Eddie's mother?"

"Eddie probably lied and said you hit him first. Then he promised to be a good boy and stay out of fights. He know they don't suspend you for being drunk, long as you don't fight."

On Saturday Marcus and Ron worked all day at a grocery store on Third Avenue, around the corner from where Ron lived. Marcus came in Saturday evening and gave his mother fifteen dollars.

"Where you get this?" That was the first time she had talked to him since Thursday, when she had to take him back to school.

"I work today, Mommy, at the market on Third Avenue."

"How you get the job?"

"My black, red-eye friend you don't like told me about it."

"You too fresh. Is only your best interest I have in heart and mind, Marcus. You must make a lot of money."

"Twenty dollars."

"And you giving me fifteen? Here boy, I won't take all your money. It's the first bit of change you make here."

"No. Keep it."

"Take half, Marcus."

"No, Mommy. You keep it."

He felt like a big man as he turned on his heels and left the kitchen. On Sunday afternoon he put his five dollars in his pocket and went to the Bruce Lee movie with Ron.

Ron took him to a theater on West 42nd Street. As they came up out of the Eighth Avenue subway and walked over to Times Square, Marcus thought Ron had led him into the middle of a hellhole.

All around him Marcus saw people who looked as if they had been recently formed by some rough, insensitive hand. Black, white, Spanish—they all looked alike, from the blackest black to the whitest blond. The ugliness, dirt, and horror of their street lives glazed their eyes and weighed their bodies, as if some force heavier than gravity kept them bound to the sidewalk.

Ron grinned, "Hey, Home Boy, ain't this something else? I know you never see nothing like this on that island of yours, but we won't get to the next corner if you don't stop looking like you just came off the boat. We got to look like we belong, blood."

Ron turned his cap backward and fell into a hipster walk that swung his whole body to a secret melody. Marcus fell in beside him, swinging to the same silent tune.

Marcus didn't find his voice until they got to the movie. "What the hell was that?"

"That's the strip, man. Forty-second Street. I know how

you feel. The first time I saw it I wanted to go back down south."

Marcus walked into the Bruce Lee movie feeling as if he'd already kung fu'd his way down 42nd Street.

Marcus saw Cassandra on Monday. She had been absent Thursday and Friday when he returned to school. She seemed happy to see him.

"Marcus, you get in trouble with your family?"

"No. Everything fine, Cassie." They were having lunch in the cafeteria and at least five students walked by him and said, "Hello, Jamaica." Cassandra smiled.

"Eddie's not back yet," she said. "Why did you fight him?"

"He insulted me."

"You couldn't ignore him?"

"No. I can't let him insult me."

"He's a fool. Everyone knows that. Was probably drunk too."

"Now he feel like the fool he is."

"You don't have to prove anything, anymore, . . . Jamaica."

"Cassie is vexed now." He reached for her and she pulled away from him. "I go' try and do better now. I'll even go back to that retarded class." He'd decided to make his life as easy as possible while he bided his time in school until he found a real job.

"Why didn't you get that business with the math class straightened out when your parents were here?" Cassandra asked.

"That's what I was going to do when I got into the confusion with Eddie. The teacher must see sometime that I know the work and then teach me what I don't know."

"Don't count on it. I could show you what we do in class

now. Maybe Schwartz will let you take the test again, and if you pass you can come back to the regular class."

"Okay, Cassie, I go' let you help me." He pinched her waist. "What else you go' show me?"

She smiled slyly. "Only some math, Marcus."

After school they went to the library. Marcus wondered why she didn't take him to her house, but he didn't want to embarrass her by asking. As he sat with her in the library he almost wished he'd listened when he was in school in St. Cruz. He vaguely remembered one of his teachers showing them the operations for algebra. But even now, as Cassie showed him how to do the problem, he wondered what purpose it was for. It was useless information for him, since he planned to be neither a mathematician nor a scientist.

But he was happy sitting in a quiet corner of the library with Cassandra. They went there on Mondays and Wednesdays when she didn't have to baby-sit. At first she tried to teach Marcus how to do simple algebra. He wasn't difficult to teach, but somehow the math became less important than their quiet conversations. For both of them it became an easy, soft time in which they escaped the harsh Bronx streets and the cold institutionalization of school.

Cassandra told Marcus about her aunt and uncle—the only family she had; the times that she lived with foster families and had run away; her dream of becoming a nurse. Marcus talked to her about the beauty of his island and told her stories about his friends and their adventures; he talked of his grandmother, whom he still missed.

They always sat at the same table, which was in a small alcove beside a narrow, barred window. They shared their dreams, dreams that went beyond the vacant lot and chunks of concrete outside the window. Marcus would never forget those times he and Cassandra sat at that table in the library on dull, winter afternoons. They were among the happiest of his life. Slowly, out of those quiet talks, they reached out for each other.

Each day, what happened in his present surroundings became more important to Marcus. Because of his relationships with Ron and Cassandra, he could think about his friends back home without feeling pained and hurt.

Eddie didn't return to school for the rest of the month and Marcus tried to stay out of trouble. He still hated social studies. They were studying the American government, and the words in the book were as long and confusing as the nonsense his tutor back home had tried to teach him. Cassie helped him with the math, but he wasn't going to tell her that he was having trouble in social studies too.

Marcus was a straight-A student in his English class, though. He'd been placed in a special English class with other foreign students, most of whom were Spanish speaking. There were also one Arab and two Chinese students in the class. The work was simple.

One day Marcus said to the teacher, "I speak English, is all I ever speak. This class for people who speak other language."

The teacher was a middle-aged woman. Marcus thought she was one of the few teachers in the school who looked the way a teacher was supposed to look. She always wore a suit and comfortable shoes, and her hair was tied tightly back in a neat bun. She smiled sweetly at Marcus.

"Sit down, dear," she said.

He wondered what was coming.

"Marcus, you'll be much better off in this class until you get used to things. Your English, well, it's not exactly the way we speak in America."

"But, Miss, it English all the same. Everyone understand me."

"I know, but you really should stay here with us, dear. You'll have such a hard time in the regular English class."

Marcus almost laughed in her face. She was like a character in one of those thriller movies he watched on television. The loyal, conniving servant trying to lure the innocent victim into remaining in the monster's castle. He stayed because he wouldn't have to work hard to get a good grade.

The economics class was impossible. He went for the laughs. Sometimes he felt sorry for the teacher, but he couldn't help joining in the loud laughter every time the man opened his mouth and the rusty voice came out. Some student was always harassing the teacher. Marcus never bothered the man. He always made sure his attendance was taken and during a point in the class when the confusion was at its height he'd slip out of the room. If he ran into Ron they'd go somewhere for a smoke, or he'd sit in the study hall with Cassandra, since it was her study period.

Marcus was becoming one of the best basketball players in the gym class, because of his practice with Ron. Now that the weather was cold he and Ron went to a community center to practice ball in the afternoons. His mother said, "Marcus, I see you is becoming a real Yankee. You don't like soccer anymore?"

"Mommy, who I go' play with, meself? Where I is now, you must know to shoot baskets not kick balls."

His father and mother were busy most of the time. They recognized, however, that Marcus seemed happier. And there were no more letters from school. His mother still worried, though. "Marcus, I pray you don't get involved with these wild teenager here."

81

His father would say, "Leave the boy. He have to have some kind of friends. I just hope he have sense enough not to take up with no thieves and vagabonds, like he did back home."

Eddie came back to school the first week in December, but he and Marcus managed to avoid one another. As it got closer to Christmas, Marcus found himself thinking more about St. Cruz than he had for some time. The Christmas holidays were always a joyous time on the island. There weren't many presents, but everyone celebrated. People visited one another, there was good food and parties.

Marcus wondered what the holidays would be like in New York. He was only sure of one thing—they would be cold. He never knew it was possible to feel so cold and still be alive.

He had no money to buy Cassandra an expensive gift for Christmas. He had hardly enough money to buy his parents a present. He heard the other boys talking about what they were giving their girls: coats, gold chains, dresses, shoes, money. He told Ron, "I wish I was back home. I could buy my girl any little thing and she happy, man."

"Look, Home Boy, you got to get in a fight with your girl just before Christmas, then you make up after the holidays is over."

Marcus laughed. "Man, I serious and you making joke."

"I got two women and you know I can't be buying two gifts for two girls. Anyway, Jamaica, them dudes be lying about what they giving their girls. They couldn't buy a subway ride. We can go to some of them shops on Third Avenue. They hire people for the Christmas holidays."

They got full-time temporary jobs in a clothing store on Third Avenue, after lying about their ages and claiming to be out of school. Marcus got to the mailbox first when the letter came from school regarding his absence. The only problem was that he missed Cassandra. He called her at home and told her he was working.

"But Marcus, you missing a whole month from school."

"No I ain't, Cassie. December is a short month. And it ain't much happening in school. You said so yourself. Everyone is getting ready for Christmas."

"You have to take off a whole month from school to get ready for Christmas?"

"Yes."

"Marcus, I don't want to see you get messed up. Looks like everyone I care about is in trouble."

Marcus and Ron worked hard and both made a hundred dollars a week. It was the most money Marcus ever had at one time in his life. One afternoon he said to Ron, as they carried in racks of clothes off a truck, "I beginning to see why people come to New York."

"Why?"

"You can make money here."

"Man, this is chump change. Don't you know that?"

"Bon, you know how much this hundred dollars is worth back home?"

"It ain't worth shit here."

The holidays weren't as awful as Marcus had anticipated. Rudy worked a lot of overtime in order to have money for Christmas. He and Louisa sent boxes of presents to the children back home, and they had some friends from Brooklyn over for a Christmas celebration.

Louisa had been cooking for days, and the guests also brought food. They had dishes from the island—pickled pigs feet, yams, breadfruit, fruitcake soaked in rum, peas, and rice. They also had traditional American fare—ham, turkey, potato salad. There was rum, Scotch, eggnog, beer, and punch. Listening to the familiar accents of St. Cruzans, dancing, singing, and sneaking drinks when the adults weren't looking, Marcus felt as if he were back home in St. Cruz. His mother and father were happier than he had ever seen them here in New York.

When school reopened in January, Marcus gave Cassandra her Christmas presents—a pair of small, gold hoop earrings and a bottle of perfume. He gave her the gifts as they sat on the bus.

Marcus had called her during the holidays, but she seemed reluctant to invite him over, so he didn't insist. She was so happy about the gifts—like a little girl. At that moment he would've tried to give her anything she asked for.

Marcus saw Eddie again after the Christmas break, too, but felt no threat from him. Eddie had lost his edge. Marcus was Jamaica now, and no one dared to bother him. Yet, sometimes he still imagined that Eddie might be waiting for him in the shadows of empty halls and staircases.

By his sixteenth birthday in April, Marcus was muscular and had grown two inches taller. His complexion had lightened since he left the island, and his smooth tan face was a perfect frame for his amber eyes that sparkled and danced, except when he was sad.

He was often sad when he was in the apartment. There was so much expectation in his mother's eyes that he knew he wasn't living up to. He hated himself for using her as a buffer between him and his father, but he didn't know what else to do.

Rudy was angry most of the time, Louisa was usually tired, and Marcus was constantly reminded in that apartment that something was wrong. They didn't feel like a family anymore. His mother tried to make their apartment look like the house in St. Cruz, but the little palm tree pictures and artificial flowers never looked right. The only time they'd been truly happy in that apartment was at Christmas. Marcus often wished something would happen to bring back the joy of that time.

Marcus still hated school, but halfheartedly tried to function there. He told himself he was doing it for the women in his life—his grandmother, his mother, and especially for Cassandra. Marcus and Ron worked in the grocery store when there was something for them to do. Most of the time there was nothing.

The end of the school year neared and even among the hulks of buildings and piles of bricks in vacant lots in the Bronx, the air assumed a springtime sweetness. Spring brings change, and change was coming.

One beautiful Saturday morning in May Marcus's mother was fixing breakfast. She opened the windows and pulled open the gate of the fire escape window. The air was fresh and sunny. Marcus enjoyed looking through the window without the bars of the gate blocking his view of the sky. There was only a flattened pile of bricks across the street from their building, so he could see clear to the next block. And the two large pots of red geraniums that his mother put on the fire escape reminded him of flower gardens in St. Cruz.

"Marcus, next month school is done," his mother said. "I glad you seem to be adjusting, but I hope those grades is better than what I saw on that last report card. I never see so much C and D in my life."

"Mommy, I trying. But wait. You didn't mention the A in English."

"You been speaking English all your life. You should get A."

"Well, me ain't speakin' American English. Me speaking St. Cruz English. It's A in American English I have."

Wiping her hands nervously in her apron, she ignored his

joke. "I wish I had time to see what really going on with you and them books. But Marcus you the eldest and you have to be a good example for your sisters and brothers."

"When they coming?"

"I don't know. They don't have papers in order yet. Me and your father still scraping and saving money to get them here. And you know we have to move when they come. This apartment can't hold eight people. Though I think them people who live over us manage to squeeze fifteen people in theirs."

Marcus smiled. His mother could always find someone who was doing worse than they were. He wondered how his five younger brothers and sisters would adjust. One brother was very quiet. He'd do well in school. Marcus thought of telling her that the other children might be better off remaining back home, but she'd only get angry. "We fit eight people in three rooms back home," he said.

"It seem different here. Seem as though we had more room. But you and the two boys could sleep on the couch when it's pulled out. And the girls—maybe I could get a high-riser for them."

"Where you go' put it?"

"In the living room."

"When you pull the couch you ain't go' have room to pull the high-riser."

"We find a way. We always do. The main thing is that we all together again."

Rudy walked into the kitchen. "I smell that codfish in me dreams and I thought I was back home."

Marcus realized that he hadn't seen his father in almost a week. He looked tired. Marcus ate silently and quickly so he could hurry from the table. Rudy had spoiled the relaxed mood merely by walking into the kitchen.

His father looked at Marcus. "Well how the big-time ball player? You know I ain't bring you all the way to the United States to learn basketball alone. Every black boy in this country know to play basketball."

Louisa interrupted. "Marcus passed all his subjects."

"I glad. One time I thought all he was passing was gas."

Marcus listened painfully as Louisa tried to make light conversation with Rudy. No matter what she said Rudy used it as a springboard to express a complaint. "I tired of these two jobs. Is a shame a man have to work so hard to make a piece of living."

"You is the only one working in this house?" Louisa asked. "How you think I feel? You think I like taking care of some-one else's children and can't see me own?"

"I know you working too! If you want to complain, then complain. It make you feel better," Rudy said.

Marcus tried to keep on eating quickly but the food stuck in his throat.

Louisa left the table and walked over to the sink. "Why complain to someone who don't care? I may as well complain to the wall."

"Is only the wall go' be left in here for you to nag because I go' if you keep harassing me!" Rudy put the cup up to his mouth and quickly finished his coffee.

Louisa clanged and banged the pots in the sink as she an-grily washed them. "That's what you want. Any excuse to be with your women."

Marcus kept his face over his plate. He couldn't look at either of them. This was the first time he'd heard Louisa accuse Rudy of seeing other women.

Rudy pushed the plate of half-eaten codfish away. "You go' dig up that dead dog again?" he yelled.

Marcus got up and left the kitchen. Rudy and Louisa were

usually like a comedy team when they fought. Their arguments were more like jokes and jibes directed at each other for the entertainment of an audience. When they were all in St. Cruz, Marcus and his sisters and brothers enjoyed listening to their parents argue because it was amusing.

However, it was one thing to argue about money, children, life in New York or St. Cruz; arguing about other women was something else. Marcus's eyes darkened as he left the apartment. This argument was not going to be funny and he didn't want to stay around to hear it. He had his own problems.

□13□

A leg and an arm flashed across the screen. Bodies that had been hurled into space came down kicking. Marcus wondered how far the movie had progressed. He and Ron must have seen every kung fu movie ever made. In St. Cruz a movie was a sometime treat, but in New York you could go every day and see a different show.

An old man sitting behind Marcus snored loudly. Marcus fished for a cigarette. The smell of stale popcorn and tobacco sickened him. Except for the coffee in the luncheonette, he hadn't eaten all day. The man's snoring was annoying. Marcus changed his seat.

Images still careened and yelled across the screen. Marcus couldn't follow the story. He wished for a quiet movie, the kind Cassie liked. A love story. He used to tease her about those movies. Cassie would say, "All you have to do is walk down any of these streets and you see the same thing that's in those old fighting movies you look at. I want to see something different."

Cassie was always trying to catch hold of something else besides what she had. She tried to make Marcus see and grab it with her. But he was a man. Women were different. He had to do what was right for him.

□14□

On the last day of school everyone was wildly happy. Marcus, Cassandra, and a group of students rode home on the bus. Ron looked at Cassandra and winked as he walked down the aisle. "Hey, Jamaica, you coming by this afternoon?" he asked Marcus.

"Yes. I coming later."

Cassandra frowned.

"What's wrong with you, girl?" Marcus asked. "Everybody happy and you sitting there like you about to draw your last breath."

"Nothing's wrong. Sometimes Ron gets on my nerves, that's all. You and him sure are tight now."

"So. Anything wrong with that?"

Cassandra adjusted her blouse. "My aunt said you can come to visit me, but only when she's home."

"She finally give in."

"Guess you won't even have time to see me now, since you so busy with your friends."

"Cassie, I getting vexed. Ain't nothing wrong with Ron."

"I didn't say anything was wrong with him. He just don't care nothing about school and you're getting to be the same way."

"Cassie, I think your mind getting rattled. School over for two months and you still worrying."

"You need to go to summer school. Then in the fall you'll be in better classes."

"God, woman, stop harassing me!" Marcus turned away, a disgusted expression on his face. "I going to make some money this summer."

"You've changed, Marcus. I used to think you was different from the rest of these boys. But sometimes you seem so wild. You wasn't like that when I first met you."

He turned back to her and put his arm around her shoulder. "Cassie, how I go' survive in New York acting like I some kind of punk."

"You so smart, do what you want. I was just trying to help you." She stared out of the window.

"Help what? You think I come from some kind of jungle where people doesn't read or write? It's a waste of time. How you know this school even giving you the right books?"

She continued staring out of the window as she answered him. "I know you got that mess from Ron. It's just an excuse. I know I ain't getting the best education, but you ain't getting any at all."

"I'm getting a job. Me and Ron."

She turned around quickly, looking at him as if he were crazy. "A job doing what?"

"Making money."

She sighed deeply. "Do what you want, Marcus. I know it's hard, but you don't even try anymore. When I came to this school I couldn't read more than fifth grade. But I worked and worked because nobody ain't gonna keep me ignorant. And nobody cares about me so I have to care about myself."

"I care about you, Cassie."

"If you care then you won't mess up."

"Cassie girl, why you fighting me? I want to work—to make money. That's what my parents come here for. To make money. So what I doing in school? I want to make some money too."

"You know your parents ain't just come here to make money. They want you to go to school. And what about your promise to your grandmother? You told me you promised her that . . ."

"I know. Cassie, in September I go' make a fresh start."

Marcus loved Harlem in the summer. People sat on stoops, leaned out of windows and lounged in front of small candy and grocery stores practically all night. It didn't matter that it was dark out. The streets had their own vibrant life. Whole families were outside escaping their hot, stuffy apartments.

One night Marcus and Ron walked along 125th Street. They'd been visiting a friend of Ron's. Marcus said, "If you take away these big buildings and put some palm trees there, it just like St. Cruz. The people look the same. And when it hot they does sit out all night in St. Cruz too."

Ron wiped his forehead. "It's hot as hell. You know down south it be hot too, but the air don't stink. It's fresh."

"The air here feel heavy, man," Marcus said. "Like it sitting on top of your head. That remind me of home too. Except there you smell jasmine and sweet William and the sea. Here you does smell shit and gasoline."

"Who the hell is sweet William, man. And why is everyone smelling him?"

Marcus laughed. "Is a flower called sweet William."

Ron said, "That's a hell of a name for a flower."

"St. Cruz is a hell of a island. I'll be glad when we get them summer jobs, though. My father say it have nothing but jobs and money in New York."

"That's what my father thought too," Ron said. "And he killed hisself trying to get up north to find it. But forget that. We got to be downtown early tomorrow. I hear there be a lot of people looking for them summer jobs."

"I wish we could get regular jobs. All-year jobs," Marcus said.

"We still in school."

"Ron, I so tired of school and my father. I could be on my own, if I had a job."

"This summer job ain't gonna help you do that. At least you have a father."

Marcus said nothing. He couldn't expect Ron to understand how it was with him and his father. They walked silently along 125th Street. At the corner of Seventh Avenue someone called them.

"Hey, Ron, Jamaica. Where you going?"

It was Charlie, a boy from school. His skinny, short frame leaned into the shadows. "It ain't nothing," Ron said.

"Hey, tomorrow me and John and some other people are getting together a barbecue in my backyard. Y'all come over."

"What kind of backyard you got? You don't live in no private house," Ron said.

Marcus laughed. "It a private house. Some abandoned building that only he living in."

"Hey, a backyard is a backyard," Charlie said. "There's one behind the building I live in. It'll cost you two dollars a head. All the food you want. You must pay extra for drinks and anything else." He grinned and poked Marcus in his ribs.

"Two dollars? I can go home and get some of the best food in the world free," Marcus said. He sucked his teeth loudly and looked bored.

"That's right," Ron agreed. "We looking for summer jobs

tomorrow and you telling us about two-dollar barbecues."

"Summer jobs where?"

"You know those city jobs students get in the summer."

"Y'all must be kidding. You know those ain't no real jobs. They just paying you to keep you off the street." Charlie's thin face lit up with amusement.

"It's better than hustling two dollars off some barnyard barbecue," Ron answered.

"Hey, I'm just doing that for fun. I got a real job. Now if you guys want to make some real money, let me know and I'll turn you on."

"Make money how?" Marcus asked.

Charlie winked at Ron. "Selling that good stuff that makes people high and happy."

"Look, I ain't come all the way to this country to do time," Marcus said.

"Jamaica, don't be naive," Charlie said. "The people I work for is pros. Anyway, how old are you?"

"Sixteen."

"You ain't gonna do no time. Not for selling a few little loose joints. The worse could happen is they put you in some rehabilitation place for a few months."

"How much money we gonna make?" Marcus asked.

"A lot."

"Tell us how much, then we be convinced," Ron said.

"Hey, I don't have to convince nobody. You know it ain't hard to find someone to deal, because everyone knows there's a lot of money in it!" Charlie leaned back in the shadows again and looked at his watch. "I got to go. Like I said, when you get tired of picking cotton, come go fishing with me."

They watched Charlie bounce off down the street. Marcus turned to Ron. "What you think about that?"

"Charlie look raggedy, but he always has a lot of cash on him. He's the biggest dealer in the school."

"I ain't know whether I should get into anything like that."

"I'm thinking seriously about Charlie's offer," Ron said. "I need the money. You got a mother and father and it's just you at home. My mother ain't got no husband. She needs me to help her, man."

"You think my family don't need money?" Marcus said. "I have five sister and brother back home. I need a job so I don't have to depend on my father."

"My mother depends on me," Ron said. "I mean she really needs my help."

"I guess they does all need help."

Ron turned his cap backward. "Your father has two jobs."

"He in the land of opportunity. He have the opportunity to have two job."

They waited at the bus stop for the bus that would take them back to the Bronx. After a long silence, Ron said, "Jamaica, who we hurting? People gonna buy the stuff whether or not we sell it. It ain't like we robbing people or mugging old ladies. Jamaica, I need the money. I want to help my moms; I want to look nice; want to take my girl out; want to have some money in my pockets. I want to feel like a man— not some tired, poor chump."

"Maybe you right. It ain't like we is knocking somebody on the head. We selling them what they want. And my father won't have to support me no more."

The moment Marcus walked into the apartment he knew something was wrong. His mother shouldn't have been home at that hour. By five o'clock she was usually off to her night job, cleaning an office.

Louisa confronted him as soon as he entered the apartment. "Here come the next problem. He such a big Yankee now. Out in the streets with that red-eyed boy. What kind of example you go' set for your brothers and sisters when they come here?"

Marcus looked behind him as if he wasn't sure who she was talking to. "What's wrong, Mommy?"

"Your father left."

"What you mean. He left for work?"

"He left for good. We wasn't getting along. Too much pressure, he say."

"What? All you never get along. He must be mad." Marcus watched her nervous movements. "Where he go?"

"He move to Brooklyn."

Marcus wanted to say something, but the words locked in his throat. He hoped Louisa wouldn't cry. Then he wondered why she didn't. Weren't women supposed to cry when their men left them?

"What about the house and car he want so bad?" Marcus asked. "What about all his big dreams?"

"Maybe he get them now." Marcus heard the first crack in her voice. "He who travels alone travels fast. You know that saying, Marcus?"

He now heard the sob in her voice, and felt tears welling up in his eyes. Tears for her pain. "Mommy, let's go back home."

"How? Your brothers and sisters looking forward to coming here. What we going back to, Marcus?"

"All you argued all the time back home too, but he never leave."

Her small body crumbled. "We came here for a new life. This must be it." Now the tears streamed down her face. "We go' make it, boy. Believe me. One monkey don't stop no show, you remember that, Marcus. We won't stop living because he gone."

Even though Marcus knew Louisa needed him there, he couldn't stay in the apartment. He couldn't face his mother's tears—or his father's old bathrobe hanging behind the bathroom door. As soon as he could get away, he went for another long walk.

The next morning he met Ron. "Let's go find Charlie, about them jobs he was talking about."

Ron looked surprised. "I didn't think you'd do it, Jamaica."

They began by selling marijuana. Marcus told his mother he had a summer job working in the park. Charlie introduced them to the supplier. The man, whom they knew only as John, said, "I like you two boys. You clean. Them other boys I had turned out to be junkies. I can't have no junkies working for me."

They each had certain parks and street corners in Harlem and the Bronx where they sold marijuana. They didn't see too much of Charlie, except when they first started selling for John. It was understood that when school started Marcus and Ron would be the suppliers instead of Charlie. Charlie was supposed to be moving into bigger and better things in John's operation.

Marcus was disappointed when after the first week they'd only made fifty dollars apiece. He said to Ron, "We almost get this working in the grocery store. What happened to all this big money we was supposed to make?"

"Don't be impatient, man. It takes a little time, that's all. Some guys are out there selling and only getting ten dollars and a loose joint. Like John says, we'll be making some real money soon."

Marcus didn't complain after that first week. It was easy

money. They went out every day and sold the bags and loose joints in the morning and early afternoon.

The apartment became just a place where he and his mother slept. It had never been a real home to Marcus. Now that Rudy was gone, Louisa seemed to care only about working. She even had a cleaning job in Riverdale that she went to every other Saturday.

She said, "It so nice up there, Marcus. That's what I want for us someday. To live in a place like that."

"That's what we come here for, yes? To live in a pretty place," Marcus answered.

On Sundays Louisa collapsed in bed all day and Marcus usually went to the beach or to the park with Cassandra. It was one of the few times when they could be together. Even though her aunt said he could visit if she were there, Cassandra never invited him.

Marcus discovered that even though his father had been out a lot anyway, when he left permanently he somehow took the remnants of their home with him. Marcus's hatred for Rudy was so powerful it frightened him.

Sometimes Marcus enjoyed being the man of the house, now that Rudy was gone. He gave Louisa twenty-five dollars the first time he was paid by John. "Mommy, take this money so you won't have to do that Saturday job."

"No, I need that work. I could save the money and it go' help get them children here. Or help buy a house. Marcus, you never know what you could do by just a little saving."

Her face was tired and drawn as she watched him tying his sneakers. "Where you going so early on a Sunday?" she asked. "I know you ain't going to church."

"I going to Orchard Beach."

"How the beaches here? Is a shame I never been to a beach since I in this country."

"Nothing like home. It have more people than sand. And the water's brown."

"Why you going? Better visit your father instead."

"Mommy, for what? What I go' say to him? We ain't had nothing to say to each other when he lived here. What I go' say now?"

"He asked about you."

"Why don't he come and see us then?" Marcus finished tying the sneakers, sat up and looked at Louisa. His eyes were dark with anger. "Mommy, I hate him."

She bolted upright and made a motion to slap him, but caught herself. Tears welled up in her full dark eyes instead, and she looked like a wounded doe. "Don't you ever say that again, boy. Don't think it. You go' bring punishment on your head. That man is still and will always be your father."

The tears finally spilled over her lids and fell down her drawn cheeks. "What happen between me and him is a man-woman thing. But you his son and nothing can change that." She wiped her eyes with the back of her hand and the wounded animal look was miraculously gone. "Instead of going to some dirty beach with that red-eye boy, you better go see your father! And you better get on your knees and ask God's forgiveness."

Marcus got off the bed, picked up his bag, and left the apartment.

By the time he met Cassandra, the conversation with his mother was forgotten. Sundays were his special time with Cassie. He avoided her during the week because he didn't want her to know that he and Ron were selling marijuana.

They walked to the end of the packed beach and sat on

the rocks that jutted into the water. "Cassie, back home we don't have this many people on the whole island much less on the beach."

Her smooth, black skin glistened like a star. "You have to come out on the rocks to find some space. Some people stay out here all night."

Marcus focused on the murky water and blocked out the screaming children and the bodies of all shapes and colors that seemed to cover every grain of sand. He gazed at the long, thin horizon and felt good. He'd felt the same way looking at the horizon on the beach in St. Cruz. There was always the mystery of what was on the other side—the possibility of something beyond his present.

Cassie broke into his thoughts. "Marcus, I called you Friday but you weren't home."

"I was at work. I told you I work at the grocery store when the man have something."

"The one on Third Avenue? I walked by there too, you weren't working."

"You checking on me?"

"No. I didn't have to baby-sit. I just wanted to see you."

"Maybe I was making a delivery." He avoided her eyes.

She searched his closed face. "I asked for you. The man said you weren't working."

"Maybe I already finished." Marcus couldn't keep the edge out of his voice. "You asked for Marcus? The people don't know me by that name. I Jamaica to them!"

"What you getting angry for?"

"I not angry."

"Yes, you are. You always get your back up when I say something about seeing you during the week."

He reached for her hand and tried to lighten his tone. "I

don't want to argue. I just trying to make a little money. I go to the store when the man have work."

"What you do when the man doesn't have work? Hang out with Ron?"

"Cassie, sometime you like a little mosquito, you know? Buzzing and buzzing in a person's ear."

She smiled slowly. "You calling me a pest?"

"Yes. And I giving you a good dose of pesticide. You going in this here Orchard Beach water."

She tried to move away from him, but he was too quick for her. He lifted her up and held her over the edge of the rocks. Cassandra laughed and squealed in his arms like a little girl enjoying a good tickle. They fell, laughing, into the water.

When they came out, all the tension between them was erased. They forgot that they were at an overcrowded Bronx beach with other escapees from the cruel August heat. Marcus promised to see Cassandra the next day, so she didn't question him anymore about where he was during the week.

He got home about ten o'clock that evening. The stoop was crowded with people from the building trying to get some air. Louisa didn't wake up when he entered the apartment. How could she sleep so in all this heat? he wondered. She must be exhausted.

He called Ron and they arranged to meet early the next morning so Marcus would have the rest of the day free to spend with Cassandra. Sweat poured down his neck as he turned on the television. There was nothing but reruns and the television seemed to generate more heat. He took a can of soda out of the refrigerator and went back outside.

He didn't feel like sitting on the stoop and talking to neighbors, so he walked up 179th Street. The narrow street teemed with people. A fire hydrant was open and kids sprayed themselves and passing cars. Marcus tried to catch the feeling he'd had at the beach, but it escaped him. It was impossible to visualize the horizon behind rows of boarded, sooty tenements.

Marcus left 179th Street and walked over to Crotona Avenue. It was crowded with people also. A group of boys were at the corner, transacting some kind of business. Marcus figured they were selling drugs. He and Ron would be doing the same thing tomorrow on some other street corner. A feeling as heavy as the night air descended on him. He felt trapped by the narrow street, and the feeling frightened him.

He continued walking along Crotona Avenue trying to shake off the depression. He didn't realize how far he'd walked until he saw Fordham Road and the Botanical Garden. He could smell the trees and grass and the animal scents from the Bronx Zoo.

It was too dark to see inside the Garden, but he sat at his usual spot and willed the depression away. It lifted slowly. He fought it with thoughts of how tired Louisa was, and how much help she needed. He told himself that he was only doing the best he could. After a while he lit a cigarette and walked slowly back home. The night air was still heavy.

About a week before Marcus returned to school, Louisa shook him awake. It was a bright Sunday morning in early September. Marcus turned over on the couch and saw that his mother was fully dressed.

"You going to church?"

"Yes. And I want you to come with me."

"Mommy, you know I does get faint in church."

"You go' get unconscious if you don't move your tail. I

102

going to church in Brooklyn and I don't like going so far on the subway by myself."

"You go to work on the subway."

"Boy, don't play with me. I work in Manhattan."

Marcus pulled himself up slowly. "But Mommy, it don't have churches in the Bronx?"

"I visiting my friend's church. Come with me on the subway. You can stay at her house until we get back from church."

It seemed as if they were on the train for hours. They finally got off at Utica Avenue and took a bus to Avenue B. Louisa seemed a little unsure of where she was going. "You been here before?" Marcus asked.

"No."

"What friend is this?"

"Someone from work."

As they walked down Avenue B, Marcus kept thinking that he'd heard the name of the street before. When his mother knocked on the door and Rudy opened it, Marcus was too angry to speak.

She said, "Here, I bring your son to see you," and turned on her heels and walked back down the stairs.

Rudy said, "Louisa! Where you going? I thought you was coming to visit too."

She turned around near the bottom of the steps. "Visit for what? You ain't my father."

Rudy threw his hands up in the air and walked into the apartment. Marcus followed him. He was too shocked and angry at his mother's trick to do anything else.

They walked directly into the kitchen. The only other rooms were a small bedroom and a bathroom. Marcus sat on a kitchen chair.

Rudy turned to him. "What's going on? Your mother have to deliver you here like a package?"

"I ain't know we was coming here."

"She told me you was coming, but it look like she have to force you."

Marcus said nothing. Rudy went into the bedroom and came out with a small television that he placed on the kitchen table. Marcus watched him hunt for words. "How's school?"

"It summer."

Rudy slapped his forehead. "I forgot. But you return soon?"

"Next Wednesday."

"You want something to eat?"

"No."

There was another long silence as Rudy fiddled with the television. "Your mother tell me you working."

"Yes."

"What kind of job?"

"Summer job. Youth program."

"Where you work?"

"In the park."

Rudy went to the refrigerator and took out a beer. "What park?"

"Central."

"What you doing in there?"

"Clean up. Things like that."

"What they paying?"

"A hundred dollars a week."

"You helping your mother?"

"Yes."

"How much you give her?"

How much you give her, Daddy, he thought. "About fifty a week."

"That's a lot of money. I know you ain't bringing home a

hundred dollars after they does take out for taxes. How much you bring home exactly?"

Marcus hesitated. "About eighty-five, ninety dollars."

"You ain't know exactly? What's wrong with you? You better learn to count."

Marcus felt as if he and Rudy were trapped together in the tiny room. He knew that his silence would make Rudy uncomfortable, so he said nothing.

Rudy turned on the television. "You sure you don't want something?"

"Nothing."

"There's a game today. Guess it ain't time yet." Rudy kept turning the channels, then stopped at an old gangster movie. Marcus stared at the television as his father hunted for words again.

"So everything okay? You taller, filled out. I told you this is a good country."

What about your leaving, Daddy? You ain't go' speak on that? Marcus said to himself. He said nothing to Rudy. Rudy changed channels. The game had started. Rudy gulped down his beer and they let the television absorb their discomfort.

The following week Marcus was back in school. He and Ron sat in the auditorium waiting for their class schedules. Ron leaned over to Marcus. "Charlie told me that John is gonna give us more responsibility. We'll make more money."

"What we have to do?"

"Nothing much. John is expanding. As he moves up, we go with him. We'll be dealing with some of his other customers instead of selling joints to these little punks in the street. Nothing heavy and nothing nasty."

Marcus looked a little wary.

"Hey, Jamaica, we ain't gonna be snatching kids and put-

105

ting needles in their arms. John is a professional—a businessman."

"I was wondering when we'd see some real money."

"Soon, Home Boy. I told my mother they liked me so much on the summer job that they gave me a permanent job."

Marcus laughed. "I tell my mother the same thing. But she want to know the number of the job in case of emergency."

"What you tell her?"

"I make up a number and give her. Women does like to worry. What emergency is coming up?"

When Marcus's name was called for his schedule he walked up to one of the desks placed around the auditorium. A sudden noise drew his attention to an exit. Eddie stood there with a drunken smile on his face, talking to two girls.

Marcus tensed up when he saw Eddie. No change in that fool, he thought. Drunk on the first day of school.

Marcus and Ron quietly and professionally supplied the school with marijuana. Sometimes they had other students make the actual sale, giving them two dollars and a joint. Some teachers suspected, most students knew. No one could prove anything.

Sometimes they delivered packages to various Bronx addresses for John. Marcus noticed that John was always a little nervous when he sent them on the errands in the Bronx. He never told them what the neatly wrapped packages contained. They assumed it was hard drugs. They got two hundred dollars apiece when they made a delivery.

Now that school had started again, Marcus was concerned that Cassandra might find out what he was doing. She'd heard from another student that Marcus was dealing. She confronted him one evening, when Louisa had gone to her night job and they were alone in Marcus's apartment.

"Tell me you ain't selling marijuana," Cassandra said.

"I'm not, Cassie. I told you that before."

"I ain't going with no pusher. I'll leave you. I mean it."

Marcus wanted to tell her that selling marijuana was not the same as pushing drugs. He also wanted to make half a confession—to tell her that he only sold it when he needed money. But the one loss he couldn't take was Cassie. He was sincere when he said, "Cassie, I don't know what you heard, but I ain't no drug pusher. You the only good thing that happen to me in this country. Don't leave me."

"I love you, Marcus. But I ain't staying with you if you dealing in drugs."

"I'm not, Cassie."

After that conversation, Marcus made sure he never sold anything directly to students in school. He had a couple of students he trusted make the sales for him.

Louisa continued to work two and a half jobs. Once she questioned Marcus when he walked in the apartment wearing a new, expensive jacket and carrying a small color television, which he said was a present for her.

"Marcus, where you getting all this money?"

"Mommy, you know me and Ron work all weekend for this man who have a moving company. We made some good, good money."

"You spent it all one time, then."

He hugged her and laughed. "No, I get the television cheap. A man needed money fast."

"Marcus, I worry about you. You on the street and I working. I don't know what you doing. And another letter came here from school about absence."

"Mommy, I trying to help you. When I can, I take work with the moving man. I want you to stop the Saturday job."

"No. I want you to stop this moving man job if it keeping you from school. We bring you here to go to school. I ain't working hard like this to see you on the street."

"Mommy, look, I stay in school. But I want to help you!"

"Marcus, you help me by not giving me cause to worry."

After that conversation, Marcus made sure he got to the mailbox before his mother did. Nothing further was said about what he was doing.

When the Christmas holidays came that year, Marcus reluctantly visited his father again. He hadn't been there since that Sunday in September.

The mood was not as strained this time because it was Christmas Eve and Rudy had company. Louisa had bought a shirt for Marcus to give to his father for a Christmas present. She'd been bugging him for two weeks to buy his father a gift, but he refused. When Marcus walked into the tiny kitchen, Rudy and his friends were drinking and Rudy was holiday-happy. Marcus didn't know whether it was the Scotch or whether he was actually excited about getting a gift from Marcus.

Rudy's face beamed as he showed off his shirt. "Look what fine taste the boy have. This my eldest boy. Handsome, just like his daddy."

Marcus remained for half an hour. He'd promised Louisa he'd visit Rudy, but he hadn't said how long he'd stay. As Marcus stood at the door Rudy said, "You looking prosperous, boy. A real New York Yankee, now. How you afford such expensive boots and a three-piece suit? That shirt you give me ain't cheap neither."

"Mommy buy the shirt." Marcus stared directly into his father's eyes and rejoiced at Rudy's surprised and slightly hurt look.

"I see. She still have to do everything for you. She buy you them expensive boots and suit too?"

"I been working."

"Doing what?"

"Helping a moving man. Working in a grocery store."

"All the money going for clothes? You ain't helping your mother? She even have to buy presents for you to give?"

Marcus's eyes darkened. "I help her. I have to go now."

Rudy squeezed Marcus's arm. They were nose to nose. "You smelling yourself, boy. I coming up there to the Bronx and I go' find out what's happening." He let Marcus go, and without saying anything Marcus started down the stairs. Rudy yelled, "Wait, Marcus. I have a Christmas present for you, and I buy and pay for it myself."

Marcus ignored him and continued down the stairs.

Rudy never got to the Bronx. He called a couple of times, but Marcus wasn't home. Louisa stopped Marcus one Saturday morning when he was on his way out of the apartment.

"Your father called yesterday."

"For what?"

"For what you think? To see how we is."

"If he care, why he ain't here?"

"You a poet now?"

"Yes. And every poem I sing is for me sweet mother." Marcus kissed her and left the apartment. Nothing more was said about money and looking prosperous.

Sometimes, in one of his rare quiet moments, Marcus thought about the frightened boy who had first stepped off the airplane and what his life was like now, almost two years later. He wondered how it was possible for a person to feel and be so different.

He seldom thought about St. Cruz anymore. It seemed so far away and long ago. "Back home" was still a special, almost magical, place. But he was here, and had learned to survive. And what about his grandmother—his promises to her? She belonged to the old Marcus, not to the fellow everyone called Jamaica.

Things were going well for Marcus and Ron until an afternoon late in January. John had told them he was opening up some other areas, and had promised to teach them more about the business. Marcus decided to leave school in April when he was seventeen. Louisa would be outraged, but he thought she'd quiet down when the money rolled in and she could quit working all of her jobs. Big dollar signs floated in Marcus's head. He'd be able to send for his brothers and sisters, move to a big fancy apartment or house. His future was clear. There was hope.

He and Ron talked about the limitless possibilities as they walked up John's block that bitter, cold January afternoon. They'd left school early because John said he needed them to make a delivery.

Shivering from the cold, Ron dug his hands in his pockets. "Man, I'm going to set my moms up down home. Buy her some land. Build her a house."

"That's a good idea," Marcus said. "I go' fix my mother up too."

They knew immediately that something was wrong when they knocked on the door of John's apartment and didn't get an answer. Marcus looked nervously at Ron. "Where you think he is?"

"I don't know. He told us to be here by twelve. He's always here when he tells us to come over."

There was a shuffling sound behind the door, and Ron knocked again. A voice whispered hoarsely, "Who is it?"

Marcus said, "John, that you? It's me and Ron."

The door opened slightly and the hoarse whisper came again. "Jamaica, Ron?"

Ron turned his cap backward and Marcus recognized that as a sign that Ron too was nervous. Ron made a motion to open the door, but John leaned heavily on it. "Man, open the door. What's the matter?" Ron said.

"Listen, y'all get the hell away from here—now! There's been some trouble. I'll contact you when everything settles down."

Marcus said, "John let us help you. . . ."

They heard footsteps pounding up the stairs. "Get away! Go up to the roof!" John whispered desperately. He slammed the door. Marcus and Ron ran to the next landing and froze as they heard the footsteps stop at the floor under them. Whoever it was kicked open a door. When they heard the animallike howl and an explosion of shots they knew it was John's door that had been knocked down.

Marcus and Ron leaped up the stairs three and four at a time. Ron looked like a tall, skinny bird. His long arms beat the air as if he could force them to be wings. Marcus's legs turned to jelly. He didn't even sense that he was moving.

They opened the door to the roof and ran across to the next building. Marcus started to open the door to that roof and go down. Ron stopped him. "This too close!"

They ran across two more roofs and came down a fire escape that faced the back alley. They jumped off the last rung and slid into some garbage cans. Ron was doubled over and at first Marcus thought he was trying to catch his breath. He then realized that Ron was sobbing. Marcus wanted to touch him, to comfort him, but he couldn't move. He clutched his aching side and leaned against the dirty brick wall.

They remained in those positions for a long time—crying and aching for each other—oblivious to the biting cold. Marcus moved first. He shook Ron gently. "Stop it, Ron, man. Please, stop. Jesus, I never hear such a sound coming out of a human being's mouth."

Ron wiped his face with his jacket sleeve. He looked like a frightened little boy. "I feel sick, Jamaica."

"Don't call me that. I done with that too. My name is Marcus."

"I feel sick and unreal," Ron whispered.

"This is real. You wasn't dreaming. Oh lord, Ron. I finished with this business. I cleaning up my life."

Ron wiped his face again. "We almost died," he sobbed.

"We was dead, Ron. But I coming back to life. I done with this."

He and Ron didn't have a chance to speak to each other about what had happened until a week later. Both of them had saved every clipping from the newspapers that told of John's murder, and they went over them together. The story was usually on one of the last pages: "Harlem Gangster Gunned Down."

John was described as a small-time hoodlum who was trying to deal in hard drugs. Ron said, "The way the papers tell it he was a punk. He was nothing."

"The papers lie about everything," Marcus answered. But Marcus knew. They both knew. John was a petty hustler. Marcus felt like a fool when he thought about his fantasies of making a lot of money working for John.

Marcus had stayed home from school the day after the incident, telling his mother he had the flu. He was chilled and couldn't eat. Louisa stayed home from both of her jobs that day. Marcus looked sick and drawn; he was grateful for her company. He didn't want to be alone with the sounds of the howls and shots still plaguing him.

Marcus went back to school two days later, but Ron wasn't there.

Cassie said at lunch that day, "Marcus you still look sick."

"Cassie, let's go to the library after school."

She opened her eyes wide. "Library? You must be sick."

"I have to talk to you."

The table where they used to sit was unoccupied. After they sat down Marcus told Cassie the whole story. "Cassie, I sorry," he said. "I lied to you and my mother." His voice trailed off.

Cassandra stared out of the window for a long time before she answered. "My cousin died from an overdose of heroin when he was fourteen. My uncle died from liquor, that's why my aunt act so crazy. She damn near an alcoholic herself. It seem like every person I know is on something or into something. I'm not getting caught up in this mess, Marcus."

He held his face and Cassandra dug her long nails into the table.

"Charlie suckered you and Ron," she said. "He knew that guy John wasn't nothing."

"Just tell me you understand. You forgive me."

"I don't understand nothing. And I forgive, but I won't forget. Maybe you didn't know what you were doing then, but you ain't so innocent now. And the way you lied to me . . ."

"I didn't want to lose you. I go' turn my life around. I

113

going to school tomorrow and I go' do what I was supposed to do two years ago."

"I've heard that before."

"I ain't saying it no more. I go' show you. I almost died. God keep me alive for something? Yes?"

Cassandra seemed to stare through him. She was somewhere else.

"Cassie, don't leave me."

"If you sell one joint, forget about me. You see, Marcus, my daddy sold drugs."

"What? Cassie, I . . ." Marcus couldn't finish.

He moved from across the table to the empty chair by Cassandra's side. He hugged her tightly and kissed her boldly on the mouth. She tried halfheartedly to pull away. "You're playing."

"I'm not." He kissed her again.

"Marcus, they'll throw us out of here." A little smile formed around her mouth.

"I like to make you laugh, not cry, Cassie. I'll show you I mean what I say. Things go' be different now." His amber eyes sparkled playfully as he looked at his watch. "I have to go. Must retire early, so I'll be ready for school tomorrow. You can't learn your lessons when you tired."

Cassandra laughed. "Nut. You gonnna be a bookworm now?"

"Only if you cuddle between them pages with me."

When Marcus got home he called Charlie. "Man, I out of the business. Ron too. We ain't dealing no more."

"Hey, Home Boy, what happened to John was too bad. But I got another connection. Some white boys uptown . . ."

Marcus slammed the telephone in Charlie's ear.

□15□

The images on the movie screen were still jumping and screaming. A man smashed his feet into another man's face. Marcus thought about that phone conversation with Charlie yesterday. Now, watching the kung fu action, it occurred to Marcus that Charlie might have put Eddie up to approaching him in the hallway that morning.

Charlie dreamed of being a big-time operator. He couldn't just let Marcus walk away—he had to teach him a lesson, like people did on television and in the movies.

Charlie knew that Eddie became brave and belligerent when he was drunk. He probably gave Eddie some wine and talked him into hassling Marcus. Charlie was the God Brother, and Eddie his drunken bodyguard.

Marcus laughed at his own joke. But the joke wasn't funny when he thought about Eddie lying in the school corridor with a knife in his stomach. Marcus got up abruptly and left the theater.

On the street the sound of sirens surrounded him. He leaned against a fence and held his head. A second police car sped down the street. He fought panic. It was like the afternoon last month when John was shot. Marcus moved slowly away from the fence, but the panic and confusion dogged him. He fended them off long enough to recognize that he was back on 110th Street.

He continued up 110th Street and walked past the subway to an abandoned building. There were too many junkies on the stoop. Junkies. He'd never heard that word until he came to New York City. Marcus looked at the building and the stoop again. Maybe he should stand there with them. Policemen don't bother junkies. He'd be safe.

He crossed the street and walked over to the stoop. One of the men was in a deep nod, and the others stared at Marcus. Changing his mind, he ran. There was another abandoned building at the end of the block. He went inside and scrunched himself in a small corner behind the stairway.

Marcus fought the flood of feeling that threatened to overwhelm him. Again he tried to form a plan. But water dripped from a pipe somewhere and the hallway smelled like rotting wood. It was a sweetish smell that made him think about St. Cruz. He tried to bring his mind back to the present. A real plan was needed now, not a reverie about St. Cruz. But the smell overpowered him and memories of the pink mornings and red afternoons of St. Cruz filled his thoughts.

□16□

I t was one of those burning, red afternoons in Sabia, the
capital city of St. Cruz. Marcus's father had just told him
and his brothers and sisters that eventually all of them would
move to New York.

"Your mother's going first. She have a job keeping house
for a family. Anna, Helen, Gerald, and Thomas, all you going
down to St. George to stay with your aunt. And Marcus, you
go to St. Ann and stay with your grandmother. I going up to
the country when the cane season start. When the season
over, me and Marcus going to New York."

The children cried. Marcus was glad he'd be staying with
his grandmother in St. Ann. He went there every chance he
got. His mother comforted the children. Rudy yelled. "All
you stop crying. I don't understand. Everybody want to go
to New York but you."

"They children," his mother answered.

Marcus kept quiet. By the time he was eight years old
he'd firmly decided he didn't want anything his father
wanted. He didn't care where Rudy went, he was staying on
his blue-green island.

Marcus used to look at the sea and wonder what lay beyond the horizon. He'd listen to Rudy's stories about his ex-

periences when he worked on a ship and traveled to different parts of the world. He listened to the endless stories that people told about their trips to New York City. Gold in the streets. Money. Beautiful women. Jobs. Opportunity. He wanted to see it someday, but not on his father's terms. St. Cruz would always be his home.

One of the younger boys asked, "Daddy, all we just going for a while, yes? I mean we ain't going to remain there?"

"You is hard of understanding," Rudy said sharply. "What the hell I want to come back here for when I leave? You don't know how it is in other places. The things I see when I working on that ship. All we have here is a black government. We ain't have no money. Who you see with money in this country? You see a lot of black men with a business that's making money? Our money is in white hands. I going to the white man's land to get me money back."

Louisa rocked the youngest, whimpering girl in her lap. "Man, all you talk crazy," she said.

Rudy ignored his wife and looked at Marcus, as if he were reading his mind. "Listen boy, your mother work fifteen hours a day in that hotel. I work sixteen hours a day in the gas station and we still can't afford you and your brothers and sisters. It better for us to send a few cents to your grandmother and let you stay with her. This way me and your mother could save a little on food and could work more, and . . ."

"Man, shut up," Louisa interrupted. "The children go' think they in the way."

"All of we is in the way."

"The only time you talk to the boy is to say something harsh."

"You want me to say nice things? You want me to say is

118

nice we have to leave our home, otherwise we go' damn near starve to death."

Marcus left the house. When cane season was over he'd go to some other part of St. Cruz. Or maybe he'd work his way to another island. He said nothing about how he felt and what he'd decided. Marcus knew everyone would laugh at a fourteen-year-old boy deciding his own future.

They were all at the airport a week later to see Louisa off. The younger children chattered excitedly when they saw the small jets on the airstrip. Customs, the baggage check, and the lounge were all in one small area. A tiny door led to the airstrip where Louisa's plane waited. They sat on hard wooden benches as the blades of an overhead fan swished hot air and flies through the room.

The children fired questions. "Mommy, you sending for us next week?" "Mommy, how long it take you to get to New York?"

Marcus wished they'd be quiet. He wanted to have Louisa to himself for their last few moments together. Only the fact that he'd be going to St. Ann to stay with his grandmother sustained him.

After their mother kissed them good-bye and disappeared into the airplane they cried. Marcus silently picked up the youngest, a girl of six. He had never felt so alone as when he watched his mother leave. He held the child and closed his eyes, fighting back the tears. Marcus looked at Rudy, and for a fraction of a second Rudy too looked as if he would cry. Then he twisted his face and turned to the wailing children. "All you stop it! Nobody dead!" The children only cried more.

Rudy said to Marcus later that day, "I glad to see you act

like a man and ain't whimper after your mother. You set a good example for your brothers and sisters."

Marcus didn't know what to say. He wasn't even sure his father had given him a compliment.

"Take this change and ride to your grandmother's," Rudy said. "You does travel that road by foot so, I go' rename it the Marcus expressway."

Marcus's long, bare feet kicked up little swirls of reddish brown dust as he ran halfheartedly after the bus. It was a van with long boards on the sides to sit on. This one was packed with market women who had made enough money to afford the ride back to the country. The others walked. They all had straight backs, dusty, flowered dresses, and large bundles on top of their heads.

Marcus watched the bus disappear around a curve. He preferred to walk. The vans were uncomfortable—and he could give his grandmother the money so they could buy some rolls for breakfast. Marcus looked toward the green hills in the distance. He figured he could reach the village in two hours if he walked steadily.

His bare feet glided easily over little stones and rocks. When he looked toward the soft rise of the hills he felt better. He had wanted to cry a second time when he saw his brothers and sisters piling into a neighbor's car for the drive down to St. George, where his aunt lived. And he missed his mother, even though he was always happier in St. Ann with his grandmother. But it was different knowing that Louisa had gone all the way to the United States. He'd see her when he found a job and was independent. He could visit her in New York or maybe send money for her to come back home.

"I go' beat the sun over them hills," he said to himself.

"Boy! You want to die? Don't make me the executioner!"

Marcus jumped to the side of the road. It was Mr. Rodney, one of the most successful cab drivers on the island. Sometimes Marcus ran errands for him in Sabia and made fifty or seventy-five cents.

"Mr. Rodney, you going by St. Ann? Drop me off."

Mr. Rodney's round cocoa-colored face became stern. He moved his head slightly toward the rear of the cab. Marcus saw the tourist. The sun had put a big blister on her nose and red patches on her face.

Marcus grabbed the door handle. "Just let me sit in front. Drop me as far as you going."

The tourist said, "Oh, Rodney. What a quaint, little town. Look at that little shack with the grass roof. My, it looks so African. I must have a picture."

Rodney rolled his eyes at the woman. "Take your picture."

Marcus still had one foot in the taxi. The woman got out and fiddled with her camera. Mr. Rodney grabbed Marcus by his neck.

"Boy, don't ask for a ride in me cab when you see I have a customer. All you come off the road sweating and smelling like a ram goat. Go' upset me passenger. Then I ain't go' get no tip because you done ruin up the atmosphere of me taxi."

Marcus felt as if the man were choking him. He swung at Rodney, but he was no match for the older man.

"Boy, you is a fool," Rodney said. "You going to fight I? If that woman wasn't here I give you a licking you never forget." He let Marcus go.

Marcus trembled with rage. "To hell with you and your customer."

"You little vagabond. Wait till I next catch your ass."

The tourist continued snapping pictures, oblivious to the argument. She even took a picture of one of Marcus's heels as he ran down the road. He knew his father would hear about what had happened. And Rodney would make it sound worse than it was.

Marcus hadn't meant to be disrespectful, but the man angered him. The hills were turning mauve now. He walked for another half hour and then sat down by the gate of the old Lawrence estate. It used to be one of the biggest sugar cane plantations on the island. Time and Mr. Rodney had turned it into a tourist attraction. Rodney liked to bring tourists there and show them the two remaining gray buildings, broken and surrounded by weeds.

Marcus could see Mr. Rodney now, spreading his arms and putting on his version of an English accent. "The enormosity of this establishment was renowned among all the islands."

Marcus used to laugh at the way Rodney fooled the tourists. They loved him because he made each one feel special. He had liked Mr. Rodney, too, except when the man's temper burst like a storm . . . just the way Rudy's did.

The sun slipped down the other side of the hills. Sometimes he, too, burst like a storm. Why? Was everyone like that? He couldn't get Rodney's angry face out of his head. And for the twentieth time that day the sound of his brothers and sisters crying and his mother looking so small and lonely entering the airplane came back to haunt him. He couldn't put his thoughts in words—only pictures and sounds in his mind that moved before him like images in a sad movie.

A dog dug through some garbage. Marcus felt as if he could sit there like the rubbish at the gate and let the dog push and toss him.

□17□

A big, gray rat rooted in a pile of garbage. Marcus jumped. Dogs in St. Cruz. Rats in New York. The rat stayed boldly where it was. Marcus looked for something to hit it with. He felt for his knife and remembered Eddie. The rat scrambled. Marcus got up and left the building. The seat of his pants was wet, and he wondered whether he had sat in anything.

It was completely dark now. The wind seemed to seep under his bones. Two of the junkies were still on the stoop of the other building. One of them looked as if he wanted to say something to Marcus, but the words were locked inside his heavy, drooping lips.

A plan. He was supposed to call Cassie. Get to the Bronx. No. Cassie would meet him there in Harlem. But where? A building with some junkies on the stoop? He'd go to the Bronx and get Cassie. They'd leave for somewhere—anywhere together. Marcus walked uptown. His head was clear now. He'd get the train, go to the Bronx and get Cassie. When he reached the subway entrance, Marcus thought he saw two boys from his school. He dashed down the steps.

A policeman twirled his nightstick. Marcus's hands trembled as he dug in his pocket. The cop looked at him. Marcus dug again. He had no money. Must have money somewhere. A train passed. The cop twirled and stared at Marcus. Marcus turned around and went back up the stairs. He felt the eyes of the policeman stick on his back like two leeches. Marcus dug into his back pocket. His wallet was gone.

He ran back down 110th Street to the building. He looked for the two junkies. The buildings themselves seemed to nod and fall in the darkness. He peered closely at every tenement. Then he saw the door where the glass was completely out. That was it. He walked through the door frame again and went back into the building.

Marcus couldn't remember exactly where he had sat. He only recalled the dripping sound and the smell of rotting wood that reminded him of St. Cruz. He walked over to a pile of rubbish. Pieces of junk had been there so long that a shoe and a tin can looked the same as a pair of pants. It was all a pile of filth. He walked over to a spot where water dripped from a pipe. Boards were piled up as if there had been a fire. He lifted one.

"This what you looking for?"

A young man of about twenty came out of the shadows holding the wallet. He shook it tantalizingly in Marcus's face. Marcus lunged forward. Someone grabbed his neck from behind and a heavy voice said, "Be cool, fool."

The man dangling the wallet laughed. "Let's get out of here." The two junkies pushed Marcus into a pile of wood and ran out of the room. He tried to get up, but his pants leg got caught on a rusted nail and he crashed back into the rotting boards.

□18□

"**B**oy, what you clawing the wood for? It's I who making you nervous?"

His grandmother sat on a chair outside her small house. The air was sweet and heavy. Marcus, tired after the long walk and the fight with Mr. Rodney, picked nervously at the wooden steps.

Amy Dodge was tall and bony, but her back was still as straight as when she was fifteen years old. "How you is, Marcus?" she asked. Her heavily lidded eyes looked as if they were closed. She sat like an old queen in the ancient, broken chair—a ruined throne.

Marcus sprawled on the top step of the splintered porch. He rested his arm on her lap and she rubbed his head and forehead softly. Marcus closed his eyes as the velvety wrinkles in her hand calmed him down. "Is going to be okay," she said. "One day all of you will be together again."

"Together, where? Here?

"It make no difference where, if you with your family."

"Where you go' be, Gran?"

"Here."

"Why don't you come to the States too?"

"Boy, what I go' do there? I an old woman, it won't be long before I . . ."

125

Marcus's amber eyes studied her closed face. "Long before what?"

"I ain't go' be here forever."

He moved away from her soft, wrinkly hands. "Where you going?" he asked.

"You know what I talking about."

He hated old people's talk about death. Something in his head beat against his temple.

"It's life, Marcus. We can't change it. As long as you love your old gran I live forever in your heart."

She lit her pipe and the pungent odor of tobacco mingled with the smell of goats, jasmine, and the sea that surrounded the island.

"Gran, I smell like a ram goat?"

"Where you get that from?"

"Mr. Rodney. He say I smell like a goat."

"Who is that?"

"A taxi driver from Sabia."

"Everything living has a smell."

"He disrespect me."

She laughed. "You ain't live long enough to earn so much respect. Mr. Rodney is a full man. I sure he ain't mean nothing."

Marcus took the change out of his pocket. "Gran, this is for we sweet rolls tomorrow."

"Your father give you this for the bus, but you walk?"

"Yes."

'She stood up slowly. "You is headstrong, but you have a good heart."

Marcus's friend Sellie sauntered into the small yard. His round face burst into a wide grin. "Good night, Mrs. Dodge. How, Marcus. Dudley tell me he see you."

"Yes, I just arrive," Marcus said.

"Mrs. Dodge can Marcus go to the falls with me and Dudley and David?" Sellie asked.

"All you don't stay long," Gran said. "Marcus have tutoring tomorrow."

"Tutoring?" Marcus was startled.

"Yes. For all the school you missing."

"But cane season start soon."

"We go' work out something."

"Gran, why? No one go to school now. Not even Sellie and them in school."

"Sellie and them never in school. Me nor your grandfather had school. Your mother and father just a little. I always thought my grandchildren could do better than this five month school and five month cutting cane."

"I rather work," Marcus said. "I ain't so big on school."

"You only big on mouth. I go' break this spell. Tomorrow, you go to Mr. Cannon's for your tutoring. No more discussion." His grandmother stood up. "I warning you, Marcus. Don't be with them boys all night. They need some tutoring too."

When they left the yard, Sellie looked at Marcus with a big laugh in his eyes.

"Sellie, don't you say nothing."

The two boys walked through thick bushes and grapevines to the waterfall at the edge of the village. It was a small fall with water trickling over large black boulders. This was their private spot. Here they could share a cigarette or a bottle of beer or rum without being caught.

Dudley and David Duncan were already there when Marcus and Sellie arrived. David had a bottle of rum that he'd stolen from a rum shop.

"David, you need to come to Sabia," Marcus said. "The way you know to steal you could make your fortune."

"Yeah, in Sabia they have them hotels and big stores for tourists. It ain't have nothing to steal here in St. Ann's," Sellie said. "But wait, listen to this. Marcus going for tutoring tomorrow to Mr. Cannon."

"Sellie, your mouth is big as your ass," Marcus said.

"What? Cannon? You mean the Old Goat?" Dudley roared with laughter.

Marcus fished around in his pocket and pulled out two greasy cigarettes. "All you keep laughing and you ain't go' get not a puff from this cigarette."

"Who care about cigarette. I know where to get something better," David said.

"What?"

"When it time I tell you. What about the Old Goat? He come here to the village one hundred years ago and tell people he a big-time professor. But I hear he was never no real professor."

Sellie lay on his back. "I hear he from some South American country and jump ship and stay here in St. Cruz."

"I ain't care where he from," Marcus said. "I ain't going to no tutoring."

Sellie turned to Marcus. "Listen. I go' give you some tutoring. I go' show you how to get a woman."

Marcus choked on the fiery rum. They all laughed.

"The boy don't even know how to swallow rum, what he go' do with a woman?" Dudley said.

Marcus lunged at Dudley, who got up laughing. Then Marcus turned to Sellie. "Okay, Sellie. You show me how to get a girl and make love to she."

The sun coming through the slats of the shutter warmed Marcus's face as he woke up. His head pounded from the rum of the night before. He looked over at his grandmother's empty cot and sat up holding his throbbing head.

"Marcus, come nuh? Leave the bed," his grandmother called from the yard. He opened the shutters and leaned out the window, breathing in as much of the pink morning as possible, before the day turned hot and red. His grandmother saw him at the window as she fed the chickens. "You was out looking at stars all night? Now you go' look at Mr. Cannon this morning."

"Gran, how you do me this? Where you get money for private tutor?"

"The only man who have a right to ask about me money is dead in he grave. Don't make me come in after you, Marcus. Come to the tap and wash."

Marcus leaned on the windowsill and smiled. "Gran, you can't read nor write but you is smart. I see you make sick people well with your tea. You learn that from listening to some old school master talking about Queen Victoria?"

"Marcus, I warning you."

He continued leaning out the window. "But Gran, I can read a little and I can count. No one ever cheated me out of change. I ain't going to college, why must I stay in school? I can't see all this fuss about school. I want to work and make money. I want to see some money."

"You go' see the back of my hand if you don't come under this tap. How you go' make money without a piece of paper proving to someone that you does know something? People ain't going by what you say you know."

He went into the yard and stepped behind a small shed, where there was a water tap. He took off his pants and shivered as the cold water ran down his back.

"Gra-Gra-Gran, I don't want no tu-tu-tutoring."

She flew behind the shed. He tried to cover himself. "Boy, what you hiding? Is many a day I wash your dirty little behind. You think you is a big man now. You is going to tutoring!"

He trembled and laughed when he saw the tree switch in her hand. He knew she'd never use it. She always told his father that Marcus was too old for beatings. After his shower he swept the front yard. When he finished he ate a roll and drank some hot chocolate. His grandmother sat on the large, worn couch. Marcus was at a small table in their combination kitchen, dining, living room.

After he ate he said, "Okay, Gran, I going to get your money back from the Old Goat." He laughed and ran out of the house before she could answer.

Marcus decided to go to Mr. Cannon's and then figure out a way to leave. The teacher had a large house by St. Ann standards. It was one of those homes built off the ground with a flight of steps leading up to the porch. Because the house was built high, there was room underneath to sit and cool off in the afternoon when the heat was most intense. Two goats ate grass in the front yard.

Marcus had never been inside Mr. Cannon's house and became angry when he thought of his grandmother giving Cannon money to tutor him. Maybe that was how he could afford such a big, fine home.

"Boy, what you looking after? I waiting for you."

Marcus jumped. He didn't see anyone. He looked at one of the goats. "You mean you really turned into a goat, Old Goat?" he said, softly.

"Look down here, boy."

The old man sat on a wooden folding chair beneath the house. There was a small table in front of him and another folding chair behind the table.

"Who ever hear of a big-time professor holding class under the house?" Marcus said to himself.

"Sit over there, boy," Cannon said, pointing a long, yellow index finger toward the empty chair.

Marcus stood directly in front of him. "Professor, sir, I want me granny money back. We ain't have no money for tutoring."

Mr. Cannon jerked his bald head like a chicken. He pointed the same finger in Marcus's face. "You better sit down before I throw you down!"

The blue veins on the side of the old man's head worked back and forth like Marcus's jaw. Mr. Cannon rose slightly from his seat. "You sit down, I say! You a child. What money or anything else your grandmother give me is none of your business."

Marcus saw that the skin on the old man's big head was thin and pale. He could crack that head like a chicken's egg if he wanted to. "My granny is suffering, man. And all you is taking her money."

"I never see a little black hooligan like you. You open you stupid mouth one more time and I going to bash all you teeth in."

Marcus laughed silently. He'd made Cannon lose his temper. Marcus felt better now.

A moment later someone threw a small stone under the house. Mr. Cannon was busy turning pages in a big, rusty book and didn't notice. Marcus looked under the opening and saw Sellie's wide feet going by.

"Excuse me, Professor," Marcus said.

"What you want now?"

"I have to pee."

"Go outside to the back. And hurry. You waste time."

Marcus ran out of the house and up the dusty road. He

saw Sellie waiting where the road turned into Sugar Lane. They laughed and kicked up swirls of dust as Marcus told Sellie about Mr. Cannon.

"Now, Marcus, you go' get some important tutoring," Sellie said. "You know a monkey don't mess in he own nest. So me no fool with these girl here in St. Ann. But this ain't really your own home here. So you could just hit and run, you know what I mean?"

"I stay here more than I stay in the city," Marcus said.

"I know, but officially your home ain't here in St. Ann."

"Since when you become the law, Sellie, talking about officially? This is my home, too, because me grandmother live here. And who ever heard of a monkey making a nest?"

Laughing and shoving each other, the boys ran up the road toward the marketplace. For the time being the tutoring was forgotten.

"**G**et up, boy. What you doing here?"

Marcus stared blankly at an old man.

"What's wrong with you, boy?" the old man asked. "You can't stay here. I'm the super. You got to leave."

Marcus stared at the man's bowlegs. A bowling ball could go through them without touching either limb.

"Answer me, boy. You a junkie or something? I'm the super here."

The man's raspy, alcoholic voice grated on Marcus's nerves. He held his head and tried to remember where he was and why he was there. "I was with me friend," Marcus said.

"What? Where's your friend now? Something wrong with you? You better get out of here."

"I was robbed."

"What else is new, young blood?" The old man threw back his head and laughed loudly. "We all been robbed." He sat down on a cleared spot between the dripping pipes and broken boards, settling in the space as if it were his own. He reached into his back pocket and pulled out a bottle.

Marcus stood up painfully, his head still throbbing. "You see two boys? They stole my wallet."

"I sees nothing. Stopped looking years ago." The old man pulled on the bottle of thick red wine. Marcus sat down again.

"Where's your friend? You said you was with a friend."

"I was dreaming," Marcus said. "Just dreaming."

"Dreaming? I ain't dreamed in fifty years." The man pulled greedily on the bottle again. "You want some, boy? This'll take away them dreams."

"You old fool. What I want with that stuff?"

"It's better than dope. Junkies don't live to be old as me. Here—better take some for them dreams."

"Shut up before I 'mash that bottle on top your head!"

The old man clutched the wine. His lower lip quivered. "Boy, I do my best to kill you."

Marcus looked at the watery-eyed man. He laughed. "Man, I give you one good cuff and pitch you in that pile of garbage. Nobody could tell you from a old rag."

"Don't mess with me, boy. I got something for you if you do."

Marcus saw the fear in the old man's eyes that contradicted his threatening words. The basement must be the man's home, he thought. Marcus's head still hurt too much to move. He'd rest there a while and then go to the Bronx. He sat down again.

The man put the bottle up to his mouth. When he finished he looked a little braver. "You talk West Indian, huh? You from the islands?"

Marcus held his head and ignored the question. The man kept talking. "I had a West Indian girl friend years ago. That woman was mean. The only woman I couldn't train. I left her when she put ground glass in my food." He laughed.

"Old man, be quiet," Marcus said. "I trying to think."

The man lifted the bottle to his mouth again and was silent. And in that still, dark basement Marcus found his mind returning once again to Sellie and that last year spent in St. Cruz.

134

□20□

Instead of going to Mr. Cannon's the next morning, Marcus met Sellie on the main road. "You going to get an education," Sellie said. "I'll show you how to be a real man."

Marcus smiled.

"Now the first thing, Marcus, you can't go round them girls grinning and smiling so. They go' think you foolish. First, you have to make believe you don't see them. That go' make them curious. And you can't go about hitting them and running, and scaring them, and stupidness like that. You have to act like a man. So we going walk by Sugar Lane and you go see them Dolly sisters."

"But wait, Sellie, that who you have picked out?"

"Sure. Is two of them to work on at once. You get to one through the other. I go' show you how."

"But I ain't like them. They look like two cashew babies."

"Why you care how they look?"

"I like Marie, over on Palmer Road."

"Boy, this just for practice. Look, Marcus, if you was to practice how to paint a picture, you ain't go' practice on a good piece of canvas, is you? You get an old piece of paper till you figure how you go' make your picture."

"Sellie, you is crazy. What pictures have to do with a girl?"

135

"You too young to understand." Sellie put on a pair of sunglasses. "Now, you follow me, Marcus. And don't smile. Just do what I do."

"Don't I get some sunglasses too?" Marcus put a big, silly grin on his face.

"It's that same thing I was thinking. But I ain't know if you look just right with sunglasses. It ain't the glasses that count anyway."

As they turned the corner of Sugar Lane, they saw the Dolly sisters outside on their rickety veranda steps. Their house was a smaller version of Mr. Cannon's. Elvira Dolly was shelling peas and Elva Dolly was sweeping the porch and talking to her sister. Their father sat under the house. When the boys got to the end of the street Sellie said, "You see that? I hope you ain't look at them girls but just ignored them like I did. You know they curious now and itching for us to pay them some mind."

"Sellie, they ain't even saw us."

"How you know? Ain't I told you not to look?"

"But, they ain't know I look, cause they ain't look at us, man."

"Marcus, you know nothing about woman. They does have they backs to you and still see everything you doing."

"So what we do now?"

"We go swimming."

"I mean about the girls."

"We walk down Sugar Lane again tomorrow."

When Marcus returned home near evening he stepped carefully in the front yard. His grandmother was talking to another woman.

"How Marcus, how was your tutoring?"

"Fine, Gran." He couldn't look at her and was surprised

136

that Mr. Cannon hadn't found some way to let her know what had happened. That was sure to come.

Marcus went into the small bedroom and sat on his cot. He'd give Gran all of the money he earned during cane season to pay for the tutoring. Deciding on that eased his conscience. He lay across the cot and smiled as he thought about Sellie's lessons in girl catching.

His grandmother came into the room. "What you learn today, Marcus?"

"Well, Gran, you know it's still just the beginning. We just do beginning things."

"Tell me."

"We did some counting—things with numbers."

"Like what?"

"Addition, subtraction."

"You already know that, Marcus."

"Is a review to get me ready for the big things, you know?"

"I hope you telling me the truth."

The next morning Marcus left the house and met Sellie on the road. Once again they sashayed down Sugar Lane. The Dolly sisters were shelling and sweeping, like the day before, and Mr. Dolly was sitting under the house and looking out on the road. Marcus noticed that Sellie's sashay had turned into a bandy-legged walk. He looked like a crippled cowboy.

Marcus became tired of the game. He put his foot out at just the right angle, gave his body a little twist, and moved with a slight bounce gracefully down the road. He had a tiny smile around his full mouth as he stared boldly at the girls. They looked back at him and smiled.

When Marcus and Sellie reached the end of the road they turned right and walked to the marketplace. They went past the marketwomen to the little square, which consisted of a rusty cannon and two park benches, and sat down. Marcus turned to Sellie. "Well, Sellie, now what we do? You the schoolmaster."

"No problem. Them girls eating themselves up with curiosity now."

"Let's go and speak with them."

"Boy, you crazy? You ain't see them father under the house?"

"How I could see? You tell me not to look." Marcus laughed. "Let's go back and talk with them, man. I tired of this walking and not looking."

"You see, that's why you young boys don't get girls. All you want to rush. Now let me tell you of the next plan."

"I tired of your plans. I going to talk to them ugly sisters."

Marcus ran back up Sugar Lane. Sellie was behind him. "Marcus, you a fool. We have to catch them girls in the grass."

Marcus ignored him. Sellie forgot about his special walk and lumbered behind Marcus. He smiled with relief when he saw that everyone was gone. "My grandmother say, 'God does take care of children and fools,' Marcus."

Marcus shrugged his shoulders. "I told you I like that girl Marie. I going for a bathe." Marcus left Sellie standing in the middle of the road looking confused.

The palms grew thicker and the grass thinned into stubble the closer Marcus got to the ocean. He smiled when he saw the girls playing near the water. It's a good thing I leave that foolish Sellie, he thought.

Marie, her sisters, and some friends sat on the rocks talking and laughing. Marie's skin was the color of rich, dark earth and her almond-shaped eyes were clear and bright. Her thick black hair rested in two braids on her neck. The girls yelled even louder when they saw Marcus. All except Marie. The water and sun sparkled in her eyes.

Marcus walked over to her. "How you is today?"

"I fine," she said quietly.

"My name is Marcus."

"I know. You Mrs. Dodge's grandson."

He sat beside her on the rock. "You come here each day?"

"No. Sometimes after school."

"Well, I go' start coming here every day."

The other girls walked away from the water. "Marie, we going now, come nuh?"

She climbed off the rock. Marcus said, "Why you have to go and I just arrive?"

Her almond eyes had a mischievious smile in them. "I'll be here tomorrow. This same time." She walked off. Marcus had driven the other girls into a frenzy of giggling.

Sellie met Marcus the next morning. "Boy, this is the day. We going to get them sisters. I heard that . . ."

"I have what I want. I ain't like them sisters. Marie go' meet me by the rock today."

"You lie. How you have the nerve to talk to Marie?"

"How you have the nerve to show me how to get a girl?"

"Listen, Marcus, I been looking at one of Marie's sisters. Maybe you could drop a hint? Mention my name?"

"You supposed to teach me. What a boy like I know?"

Marcus met Marie by the rock. He was happy that she was alone. She let him kiss her and hold her long, soft fingers. He wanted to tell her about his plans, but was afraid she'd tell one of her sisters or friends. Then the whole village would know he was going to run away. He remembered what his grandmother always said: "If you want to keep a secret then keep it to yourself."

As soon as Marcus arrived home that afternoon he knew

his grandmother had found out about his not going to tutoring. She held a tree switch in her hand and her eyes were small and red. Marcus stifled a smile. She reminded him of an old lion tamer as she flicked the switch in the hot air.

"Marcus, you been lying to me."

"Come, Gran. I explain." He tried to put his arms around her.

She jumped away like a young girl. "Marcus, this switch go' do the explaining."

"Come, please. Gran, listen."

She threw the switch in a corner of the yard and walked into the house. Marcus followed her.

"I should let you lick air. Food is for people who deserve it." She opened a can of corned beef and poured it over steaming rice.

"Gran, I sorry. I go to Cannon's tomorrow. Is that you paying him money you don't have that make me angry." He sat down on the couch and made his amber eyes look large and sad.

"You think the cat care when the kitten get angry? You is disrespectful and rude. You cause Mr. Cannon to walk all the way here to tell me you go out to pee and never come back."

Marcus ate quickly, in case she changed her mind about feeding him. "It take him two days to walk here?" he asked.

"I not joking, Marcus. Then you break your promise to me. You look straight in me eye and lie. That's what hurt the most."

"Gran, I sorry. I go tomorrow. But the money I make cutting cane I giving it all back to you for them stupid lessons with the Old Goat."

"You say one more rude thing and I putting you out of this house!"

"But Gran, what I say to make you so—?"

"You call them lessons stupid? You call the man a old goat? You can barely read and write and me can't read or write at all." She sat down across from Marcus at their makeshift kitchen table. which was actually a large coffee table, and picked at her food.

"I hear you and the other ladies calling him Old Goat, Gran."

She leaned into his face. "We ain't saying it in malice. And we his age. You is a child. You must give the old one respect whether you like him or not." She pointed a finger at Marcus. "The man know more than you. When you can read the books like he, then you have the right to an opinion. Is too late for me to learn, but not you. I don't want you cutting cane all your life."

"But the money. How you could afford to pay for tutoring?"

"He ain't charging me. I do him a favor once, and so when I ask him to help my grandson keep up his lessons, he say yes."

"He don't like me. He giving me lessons under the house."

She threw her hands in the air. "What you care? Some people happy to take a lesson under a tree. The man have something you need. Get it, I tell you, then dislike him all you want."

"What kind of favor you do for him?"

"His wife was sick. They were young then. She had fever and stomach pain. There was a bad storm so no one could leave the village to get a doctor. It was your grandfather who saved she. He know all about the plants. He brew her some tea and the fever break."

"Gran, you see. You is a doctor. Teach me about them plants."

"Boy, this ain't fifty years ago. This is changing times. You learn from books now. I learn about the plants from your grandfather. His father taught him. But I want you to be a modern doctor. I want you to read books."

"Gran, I take them lessons, but is only for you I go."

When Marcus reached the falls that evening he saw a strange boy with Sellie and the Duncan brothers. The new boy looked about eighteen years old. His hair grew in thick, long coils down his back and he had soft, sad eyes. Sellie said, "Marcus this is James, he one of the Brethren."

Marcus said hello. He had heard of a group of people who lived in the hills and believed in a lot of strange things. People said they were wild and violent. Most St. Cruzans hated them. What Sellie and them up to now? Marcus thought.

"You have a cigarette?" Marcus whispered to Sellie.

"Shut up, Marcus, and listen to Brother James."

The young man looked out into the black night. "As I was saying, the black man must go back to his African purity if he wants to be free. Africa—Ethiopia—is our home. Not here."

Marcus hit Sellie in the ribs. "What's wrong with this man? He look high or something," he whispered.

"Hush. We ain't want the man to think we ain't interested in what he saying."

"But, Sellie, I want a cigarette." Marcus leaned into Sellie's stone face. "I have something to tell you about Marie's sister."

"Marcus, you go' mess the whole thing up. Now shut up before I pelt you."

The young man looked toward Sellie and Marcus. "We live a natural free life, a black man's life. We live in the hills. We don't eat swine. We does make everything we wear. We

142

sell the things we make for other things we need. We don't believe in violence. But here is not our home. Here is Babylon. It's oppression here."

The boy's words reminded Marcus of his father. Oppression. That was one of Rudy's favorite words. He wondered what it meant.

Sellie pointed at Marcus. "He leaving here soon."

"Where you going?" the man asked.

Marcus frowned at Sellie. "New York."

"That's Babylon too. Is Africa where we must be."

"I thought all St. Cruzans wanted to go to New York," Marcus said.

"They don't know any better, little brother." The young man got up abruptly and walked away.

Marcus stared after him until he disappeared in the dark beyond the firelight. He was fascinated by the young stranger. "Sellie, who is he?"

Dudley laughed. "You ain't hear what the boy say? He a natural, free black man. We want to be free and black, too."

"You already black!" Marcus said.

"We ain't as free as he," Sellie laughed.

"We want some of that weed they does smoke to get free," David said.

Sellie puffed on a cigarette. "That boy is smart, though. He only a few years older than me."

"I know a boy a few years younger than you who smarter," Dudley said. Both of the Duncan brothers laughed.

"But why they wear their hair so?" Marcus asked.

"A true black man doesn't cut his hair," David answered.

"How you know?"

"That's what the man just tell us."

"The police run their behinds from one hill to the other," Dudley said.

"They illegal?" Marcus asked.

"No. The police don't like them because they is free."

"What is oppression? What do Africa mean to us? We St. Cruzans."

"I don't know, Marcus," Sellie answered. "I just want some weed so I can be free like the brother."

Marcus kept his promise to his grandmother and went to see Mr. Cannon the next day.

"Take this, boy." It was a fat, rusty, brown book. Marcus couldn't read the title—partly because the print was worn and partly because the words were too long. The professor had an identical book. It was just as rusty as the one he had given Marcus.

"Open to page twenty-one."

"Bats go' fly out this thing," Marcus muttered to himself.

"Open the book, boy. I want you to read along with me." Cannon seemed to puff up now. His voice boomed under the house as he read. "In the year 1843 Queen Victoria . . ."

Marcus relaxed. He kept his head over the book, but his eyes were on Mr. Cannon's chicken who was walking around Cannon's foot dropping little round black pellets. Marcus had to fight to control himself. He held in the laughter until tears came out of his eyes.

Mr. Cannon was still reading. Marcus heard him say something about sailing around the Horn of Africa. Marcus regained control of himself; the name Africa reminded him of the boy the night before. "Excuse me, Professor?" Marcus raised his hand as if he were in a proper schoolroom.

Mr. Cannon rolled his eyes up to the ceiling boards. "What you want now?"

"How does we come to be in this place? Is we Africans? Is we black?"

Cannon put the book down. "Let me explain this thing to you so you won't be confused. Hundreds of years ago a few Africans were brought to this island. But they weren't really slaves. They mixed with the Indians, who were the first people here. Then the Spanish, French, and English came. And those of us here now are mixed with the Indians, Spanish, French, and English. You're no African. You're a St. Cruzan. It was just a couple of Africans they brought here and they quickly mixed up with the Indians so you couldn't really tell who was who. And anyway, the few Africans they bring to the islands was like kings and chiefs and princes. They sent the riffraff Africans to the United States."

"But what about being black?"

"Marcus, I just tell you, we St. Cruzans."

Marcus stared at Mr. Cannon. Age had yellowed his skin, but he did have an Englishman's pale eyes and a Frenchman's long nose. Marcus thought about his grandmother. She was black as pitch. Maybe the combination of Indian, English, French, and Spanish blood affected people differently.

"Professor, I still confused."

"But I just explain. You have a rich heritage and history. English, French, Spanish, and all that is your history."

"What about the Indians?"

"Well, they don't have much history. They just always been here with their bows and arrows until the English, French, and Spanish came and settle them down."

"What oppression mean?"

"Marcus, you trying to get away from the book. Come back to your book."

145

On his way home from the lessons Marcus passed the market at the beginning of Sugar Lane.

Sellie ran up to him. "Marcus, you just missed it. You know that man James who spoke to us last night? Well he try and sell a wood carving to one of them marketwoman. Now what that woman want with carving? He tell she he trade the carving for some yam or plantain or something. I not sure what. The woman start up one cursing. But the man, he don't care."

Sellie acted out the scene for Marcus's benefit. "The man go to a next woman and try to give she the carving for some sugar apples. Well, this woman worse than the first. She stare at the man, and before anyone know what happen, the woman rise up and snatch the man by his hair."

Sellie grabbed Marcus by his hair and Marcus pulled away, laughing. Sellie went on, "The two of them fall to the ground and roll over where the first woman have some tomatoes. Well, Marcus, they roll over the woman's tomatoes and squash them. So now this woman is raving and she in the fight too. But we ain't know whether she fighting the man or the other marketwoman. All we seeing is arms and legs. Someone rescued the man, but his carving got mushed up in the fight and he still have nothing to eat."

Marcus could see the young man standing in front of a woman at the far end of the market.

"Go back to them hills and plant something," the woman screamed. "Then you have all the food you need. All you Brethren is just lazy."

"I got to go home, Marcus," Sellie said. "I see you later."

Marcus pushed and shoved his way through the crowd until he was close to the screaming woman and the young man. The man's large, sad eyes reminded Marcus of a skinny cat he'd brought home once. Rudy had made him get rid of it.

"You, woman, are in darkness," the young man said. "Ignorance has put a veil over your eyes."

"I go put a veil over your face and shut your lights for good if you touch one of me fruit!"

The whole market was in an uproar. The two women Sellie had told Marcus about were hurling insults at each other. Everyone else was intent on driving the man out of the market. One old man said, "If he put a hand to anything that belong to me he drawing back a stump."

Marcus picked up a handful of sugar apples and an avocado pear. No one saw him as he slid them under his shirt. Then he walked over to the young man. He recognized Marcus and together they left the group of yelling women.

When they reached the end of Sugar Lane, Marcus gave the young man the fruit. "I feel a good spirit coming from you," the man told Marcus. "Meet me here tonight. Alone."

When Sellie came by for him that night to go to the falls, Marcus said he had to do something for his grandmother. He promised to meet the boys later if he could. After Sellie disappeared into the tall grass, Marcus ran to meet James.

He didn't see him immediately and became a little annoyed. Then Marcus heard a slight rustling and saw the man leaning against a tree.

"We going to the beach," James said.

"It's a long walk."

"We can talk better there."

When they got to the beach they made a small fire. The young man's eyes dominated his small face. "I know you are of a right mind and heart," he said to Marcus. "Your friends just want some of the weed. But it's a holy weed. We don't use it for fun. I feel you're different. But you must know who you are so you can be free."

"What you mean? I'm Marcus. That's who I am."

147

"I mean you must know that you come from a great people. The African. Things happened. The African lost his greatness. We were taken out of Africa and brought to the Babylons of this world—we are in exile. We are made to feel inferior to all other people. We are oppressed."

Marcus liked the words the man used, even though he didn't know their meaning. Exile. Inferior. Babylon. Oppressed.

"What is oppressed?"

"When a foot is put in your neck and your face remain in the dust of the road."

"We are black men. African men, then?"

"Yes."

"We ain't mixed with Spanish, French, English, and Indian, which equal a St. Cruzan?"

The young man laughed. "That's the kind of ignorance been spread through this island for centuries. Little brother, look at our skins—our faces. We are black. We are Africans. And the Brethren know the way to freedom. You don't see us sick and in slavery. We live in the hills. We live a natural life. We going to find the black man's glory again."

The waves crashed against the rocks. The young man talked and swayed with the rhythm of the sea. Marcus didn't know what to make of much of what James said, but he'd found one St. Cruzan whose ideas were new and different. Things were a little clearer now. He'd work through the cane season so he could give his grandmother the money he'd made. Then he'd go to the Brethren on the hills until Rudy left for New York.

"I'll teach you about our way of life if you want to learn," James said.

"Yes. Is what I want. I want to become a Brethren.

"Marcus, you can't make a decision so quick. It takes time. First you must learn about us."

148

"My mother is in New York," Marcus said. "Me and my father is leaving to go there after cane season. I don't want to go with him."

"Marcus, what's important is what is in your heart. Keep the spirit. Even in the dark, Marcus. The spirit is there. It will see you through until you get home."

"You won't tell anyone what I tell you?" Marcus asked.

"No," James promised.

Marcus went to Mr. Cannon's the next day. He dreaded it. The hour he spent there seemed like ten.

"Boy, you ain't paying attention."

Marcus clutched the book. Whenever Mr. Cannon was angry he talked like a villager. His voice was dry and dusty, like the pages Marcus stared at.

"Boy, turn the page. You think the page turn itself?"

Marcus kept his head down and slowly turned to the next page. His thoughts were on the young man and their conversation the night before. He could listen to James's words all day even if he couldn't understand everything he said. But the words on the page were just long, black lines with white spaces in between.

"Parliamentary procedure notwithstanding, the terms of the . . ."

"Professor? I have a question."

"If it's not about what we reading, don't ask it."

"It's about the book. I want to know if it have any part in this book that talk about the African man, the true black man?"

"You interrupt me for some foolish question? This is important history I teaching you. I thought we settled that question yesterday."

Marcus slammed the book on the floor. He didn't know whether it was the chicken or Mr. Cannon who squawked when the book hit the ground. Marcus ran down the road to the end of the village and headed toward the beach. Hoping to find James, he sat down and looked at the blurred horizon. What was on the other side? His mother getting a new home ready for them? Africa? Nothing?

A bird dove into the water and came up with a small fish struggling for life in its bill. The sight frightened Marcus, even though it was something he'd seen many times before. He knew for sure that if he ever left St. Cruz he'd never see his home again. His grandmother. Sellie. The Duncan brothers. James.

He saw James walking toward him from the other end of the beach. The young man came over and talked to Marcus. The words dissolved into a chant that kept time with the crashing sea.

"I not going back to that professor," Marcus said. "My grandmother go' be upset. I promised her I'd go to the tutoring."

"You have to explain to her. That's how a man act. Tell her how you feel."

"Suppose she won't listen."

"She'll listen. Be honest."

His grandmother waited for him on the porch. She looked like a hard rock blocking the entire area. Marcus sat on a step, positioning himself sideways so he wouldn't have to look her straight in the eyes.

"Which place you was, Marcus?"

"Nowhere."

"Tell the truth." Her eyes bore into the side of his face.

"I walk to the beach."

"By yourself?"

"Yes." His face burned.

"You lie."

He turned around and faced her fully, as her eyes demanded. "No, Gran. I walk down to the beach. The professor vexed me today."

"What did you do?" Her eyes held him fast and he couldn't turn away from her, nor could he lie.

"I throw the book down."

"You mean you throw the book in the man's face?"

"Not in he face. At him foot. Gran, I sorry. I couldn't help it."

"You have to do something about the fire in you, Marcus. Else you go' spend the rest of your life sorry about something."

"Gran, please, no more tutoring. I promise, when the season is over I go' try hard in school. For you, Gran. I promise," he pleaded.

"You going to the States after cane season."

Marcus tried to keep a normal voice. "Gran, wherever I go I promise I study and make you proud of me."

"What you mean. Wherever you go?"

"I ain't mean nothing. Except I promise to do better."

"You promised before, promised to go to the professor."

"Please, Gran, the man don't like me. The book don't make sense."

"How it go' make sense when you can't read it?"

"The man make me so angry."

"You have to learn to get on with people who vex you. Don't burn in your own fire."

"Gran, please don't ask me to go again."

"I hope you don't live to regret some of the things you do. Me can't fight you. I too old now. Just apologize to the man."

"Gran, I do that for you." He got up and hugged her tightly.

Marcus went to Mr. Cannon's the next day. The old man was in his hammock snoring while several flies buzzed around his face. Marcus laughed. He the only man who have flies following him before he dead, Marcus thought. "How, Professor!" he shouted.

Mr. Cannon squirmed and opened his eyes. Marcus smiled. The old man looked as if he were surprised that he was still alive.

"What? Is you? I'm not tutoring a hooligan like you again." Cannon sat up stiffly and waved his index finger in Marcus's face.

"You ain't going to tutor me no more?"

"No!"

Marcus bowed his head. "Thank you, Professor. I sorry I throw down the book." He kept his head bowed so Cannon wouldn't see him smiling.

There were two more weeks before cane cutting. After Marcus did his chores, sometimes he'd spend the rest of the morning on the beach with Brother James. But they had to be careful. If anyone saw him associating with James the news would spread like an epidemic through the entire village. Marcus wanted to be the one to tell his grandmother when the time came for her to know.

After he spent some time with James, Marcus would meet Marie by the falls. She'd never come alone since that first time she'd agreed to meet him. Marcus figured since there were so many girls he'd tell Sellie and the Duncan brothers to come also. But Sellie said, "Don't tell them randy brothers. They go' mess things up and chase the girls away."

It was a happy and carefree time for Marcus. Laughter. Azure skies. Clear water. Sparkling, brown limbs. Sellie bouncing from one girl to the other. Passionate fourteen-year-old kisses. He'd even forgotten about Rudy's pending arrival.

One afternoon when he came in from the falls, he saw Rudy in the yard with Mr. Rodney. Marcus balled his fist and prepared for the attack.

"Marcus, you threatened Mister Rodney?" Rudy bellowed.

Marcus stared at the men. "No, Daddy."

"You was rude to this man?"

"No, Daddy."

Rodney frowned. "Cause me to almost lose a customer," he said.

Amy Dodge came out and looked at all of them, but said nothing. Marcus was relieved when he saw her. "I ain't know the man have a customer," he said.

"Apologize for what you did," Rudy demanded.

"I ain't do nothing, but ask for a ride."

"The boy put up his hands to me, man," Rodney said.

Rudy's thick hair seemed to be standing straight up. He and Marcus had the same amber eyes that captured and held the island sunlight. And Marcus was almost as tall as his father.

"Apologize!" Rudy said.

Marcus was silent.

Amy stood by Marcus. "The boy say he ain't do nothing. Ask him his side."

"Stay out of this. He my son."

"That's why he act just like you. Why he won't apologize for something he ain't do."

"How you know?" Rudy asked. "You was there? He want to be a man then he have to learn how to take licks."

"He too big for you to beat now."

"He a child still. He want to be mannish. I go' show him what a man feels."

Sellie stood in his own yard watching the scene. Rudy

pulled off his belt. Marcus, never taking his eyes off his father, backed away until he came to a bench where some tools lay. He grabbed Rudy's machete. Mr. Rodney yelled, "Oh God, man. The boy crazy."

His grandmother said softly, "No, Marcus."

Rudy froze. Marcus dropped the machete and ran out of the yard. He heard his father scream after him, "You no son of mine! I never want to see your blasted face again."

Marcus walked to the falls. Sellie followed him there. At first they said nothing. Then Sellie gave Marcus a cigarette. "What you going to do now?" he asked.

"I don't know. I can't go back to the house if he there."

"You could stay by us."

"I never want to see the man face again. It just my Gran. She go' be hurt if I don't stay by she."

"We start cutting cane tomorrow."

"I know." Marcus had never seen Sellie so concerned or worried. At that moment there was no question in Marcus's mind about whether or not he could trust Sellie. "Sellie, I go' tell you something. Promise you say nothing to a living soul."

"I promise, Marcus."

"I not going to the States. I joining the Brethren soon as the season over."

"You crazy? Is that where you was disappearing to? You been with Brother James?"

"Yes."

"But, Marcus, them people crazy—living up in them hills like they in a next world!"

"You don't understand, Sellie. All you just make a mockery of the man. You don't understand. But, Sellie, if you tell even your dog I go' do my best to . . ."

154

"I ain't go' say nothing. Quiet, here come David and them."

David Duncan sprawled on his back and looked up at the approaching dusk. "We go' have money in our pockets now, Marcus. Cane cutting start tomorrow. I go' take me a trip to Sabia out of that same money I make," he said loudly.

Sellie looked at him. "You go' make just enough money to take a trip to the market and buy your mother one fish head."

Marcus slept at Sellie's house that night. He was worried about his grandmother because he knew she was worrying about him. The next morning he sent one of Sellie's sisters over to his grandmother's to tell her where he was.

It seemed as if the entire village was at the main road that led out of the village, waiting for the ride to the cane fields. Rudy sat at the side of the road with the other men and completely ignored Marcus. Marcus stayed with Sellie, the Duncan brothers, and a group of other boys.

He was happy he'd cut ties with Rudy. Now Rudy could be any stranger sitting by the side of the road. The odor of wildflowers and lime drifted on the cool, fresh air. The mountains looked blue in the morning haze. A group of young girls whispered and giggled under a tamarind tree. Marcus had waited six months for the day when he'd hold a machete in his hands and knock down cane; when he could sit by the road digging his toes in the red dirt until the truck came; when he could watch a pink morning rise out of the blue haze of the hills.

Several trucks barreled down the road. There were already some women and men from neighboring villages on them. Everyone scrambled in. Marcus made sure he didn't get on the same truck with Rudy.

The first day was always the worst. Marcus's back was unaccustomed to the fierce sun for so many hours at a time. By the end of the day he had blisters on his back and his hands were tender and raw.

He went back to Sellie's house, and his grandmother was there waiting for him. He embraced her. "Gran, I sorry. I can't stay there with him."

"Marcus, you must talk to him."

"I can't. Who can talk to him?"

"The man ain't bad, Marcus. And he your father."

"Why you defending him?"

She stood with her arms folded and legs slightly apart. "Look boy, this ain't no prizefight. I know he have a temper, but he only doing the best he can. He love you. I know that. It just hard for him to show. And if you want him to show love you have to do the same. The road go two ways."

"How could he love someone and always be harassing and beating them?" Marcus moved closer to her, but she kept her arms folded.

"I know it hard for you to understand. But your father want so much. He always say he want his children to have everything. And he want to be proud of you. You his first son."

"He tell me I ain't his son. I like not being the man's son." Marcus pulled his eyes away from her stare.

"Marcus, he ain't mean that. You and he is so much alike, that's why all you can't get along. You could have just left Mr. Rodney's taxi, why you have to stay there and fight him? The man is ignorant, I can see that."

"But he insult me, and he grab me first."

Her feet seemed to be rooted to the spot. "Sometimes you have to lick your pride and walk away, otherwise you go' have a lot to regret."

Her eyes captured Marcus's again and he was forced to

return her stare. Those heavily lidded old eyes could see the secret places in him that no one else saw.

"I knew your father from the time he was a boy," Amy Dodge said. "He have nothing. His mother and father dead. He live with some old blind man he used to help. He was good to that old man. They were two poor souls. A blind man and a boy—helping one another keep alive. Sometimes I used to pay your father two cents to do a little errand for me. Or I give him a little supper sometime. I know that boy ain't have the benefit of a mother's softness. He was smart and did the best he could. When he and your mother fell in love I was a little upset. I mean, the boy ain't have no money and no education. But I see something in him. I know he wasn't lazy."

She unfolded her arms and put both hands on Marcus's shoulders. Amy Dodge was still a little taller than her grandson. "He trying, Marcus. He ain't a bad man. He keep his family together all these many years. And look, he give you the chance to do something with your life. And you go' have to face him one of these days. You ain't go' never be right till you face him. You can't keep running."

She kissed Marcus lightly on his forehead and walked away, across the yard.

□ 21 □

"**B**oy, what's wrong with you? What you running from?"
Marcus's head throbbed. He felt as if his body
was attached to the pile of boards he was sprawled over.
"Nothing. Drink your wine and shut up."

"Something's wrong with you," the old man said. "You got
no family? You one of them runaways?"

Marcus ignored him. He fought to form a plan. If he could
get back to St. Cruz. To Sellie. Brother James.

"I ran away once. When I was eight years old."

"Shut up!"

"Them streets gonna eat you up, boy."

"Maybe I go find Cassie."

"Trust few men and no women."

"Shut up, man, I can't think."

The old man laughed. "Think about what? Take some of
this, make you feel nothing. That way you feel better."

Marcus ignored him. Thin beams from the streetlights
came through the dirty, broken basement windows. The light
threw a sickly haze on the old man's face and the pile of
garbage behind him.

"Whatever you need boy, you ain't gonna find it here.
This place is for people like me who stopped running. Got

no place to run to. Nobody to run from no more, either. I had a boy like you once. Run from him and his mama. They needed too much. Boy needed food and clothes, the mama needed love. Guess the boy needed some love too."

Marcus looked at the old man with interest. "You hated your son?"

"No. I just didn't love him then. I love him now. Now that I ain't afraid of feelings. See when feelings get to be too much, I just take some of this."

"You an old fool."

"I know. This ain't no place for you. You better get out of here 'fore you stay forever."

Marcus thought about that. Maybe he should stay. No one would look for him here.

"You want to stay here, then keep running, boy."

"Old man, you talk crazy."

"That's what you gonna be if you don't get out of here. But if you stay, you may as well take some of this." He held the syrupy liquid in his mouth again.

Marcus ignored him. The streetlamp filled the room with a strange haze—that reminded him of something. He tried to turn away from the light so he could think, but it pulled on his mind. The old man was snoring now. The light. The snoring. St. Ann. His father.

□22□

He heard Rudy snoring on the couch in the sitting room. His grandmother breathed softly on her cot in their tiny bedroom. Anger kept Marcus awake. It was only because his grandmother had begged him that he had come back to her house. Marcus couldn't sleep under the same roof with his father.

In the morning, Marcus waited until he heard Rudy finish washing under the tap before he'd leave the bedroom. He wouldn't go in the sitting room to have his hot chocolate and bread until after his father had left the house. Each morning Marcus stood on one side of the road with Sellie and the Duncan brothers, and Rudy stood on the other side with some older men. They always rode in separate trucks. In the evening Rudy ate his dinner on the porch or went to the restaurant-bar in the square. Marcus and his grandmother ate in the house.

"Marcus, you ain't talk to your father yet."

"Gran, is only for you I come back here. I want to take care of you, Gran. Don't worry. I know what I doing."

"Marcus, I ain't go' say it again, but you and him both go' have to face each other one day."

160

Things were ending. Rudy would be going to New York and Marcus would start a new life with the Brethren. One evening, two months into the season, Marcus came in from the fields. His grandmother was in the little shed that served as a cooking area, stirring a steaming pot of fish soup. She went to pick up another pot and stumbled.

"Gran, what's wrong?"

"Nothing, boy. I just trip. Sweep the floor so me won't fall on things."

Marcus studied her closely. She left the shed and walked quickly into the house as if she were hiding something. When they ate that night Marcus was too tired to see the lines of pain and the twitching across her long face. The following morning she shook him gently. "Marcus, get up."

"What? Sellie and them looking for me?"

"No, it's morning."

"I thought it was still evening. You mean I sleep into the next morning?"

"Yes." She sat on her cot and fanned herself.

"Gran, what's wrong? You don't look just right. Why you fanning so?"

"Nothing, Marcus. Hurry and wash before you miss the truck."

She was usually in the kitchen or the yard working when he got up. Not sitting on her cot with a broom in her hand. He held her arm.

"Gran, something wrong."

"I okay. Just a little tired. I an old woman, you know."

"Let me stay and help you."

"I go' be okay."

He grabbed her broom. "I go sweep the yard."

"Marcus, you going to miss the truck."

"So. I always missing something."

She took the broom back. "I okay. Let me fix you tea. Your father gone already."

So what, he said to himself. He turned around as she walked out of the room, so he didn't see her left foot dragging. He washed under the tap. When he walked into the tiny room that served as a sitting room and kitchen, the cup of steaming tea was on the scratched mahogany table. The dark, worn wood reminded him of his grandmother. "Gran, I stay here and do for you today. You rest."

"No. I go' be fine. I just relax."

"I staying."

She sat down heavily on the couch. "Marcus, you need that little bit of change. You don't want to go to the States a pauper. I rest, and when you get back we eat a nice supper."

"How you can fix a big supper when you say you is resting?"

"I go' be okay."

"Didn't daddy see you this morning? He know you ain't feel well?"

"I not sick, boy."

He looked at the open door. One of their chickens was peeping inside. "Don't cook until I come home. Stay in bed, Gran."

"Yes, Marcus. Come, nuh? Finish the tea before you miss the truck."

He ran to Sellie's house. "Mrs. Boyd, look in on Gran, please. She don't feel too well."

Sellie's mother started wailing. "Oh God, boy. What's wrong with she? I ain't know she to be sick a day in she life."

Before Marcus could say anything else, Mrs. Boyd ran across the yard to his grandmother's house. The woman is a fool, but she'll look after her, Marcus thought. He ran to catch the truck. The Duncan brothers helped him on as it slowed down.

"Marcus, we was worried about you," Sellie said.

Marcus was surprised to see his father on the truck. They ignored each other. One of the older women made room for Marcus on the slab of wood. He wanted to tell Rudy that he thought his grandmother was ill, but he just couldn't talk to him—not even about that. He also didn't want everyone on the bus asking him questions.

Marcus worked quietly and hard that morning. When they stopped for their break, Sellie said, "Marcus, something bothering you?"

"No. I okay."

After they finished work for the day, Sellie said, "Let's go to the falls for a swim before we go home. You go' see them girls we was out there with last night. What happened to you last night?"

"What girls?" Marcus asked. "Them ugly Dolly sisters? I going to buy some things for me grandmother."

"You 'coming a granny's boy? Them sisters ain't so bad, you know."

Marcus ignored Sellie and walked to the market. He bought two sea bass, three plantains, two sweet rolls and some ground cornmeal. He then went to a little shop at the end of the market and purchased two meat patties and a bag of the coconut candy Gran liked so much. He put the change in his pocket and walked back up Sugar Lane toward home.

When he arrived, he saw Sellie's mother and father and Rudy standing in the yard looking worried.

Sellie's mother came up to him. "Marcus, your grandmother resting now. I made she some tea. Mrs. Grace sitting with her." She looked at the packages in his arms. "What you have there?"

"Dinner for me grandmother."

"Such a lot of food? The poor woman can hardly take a sip of tea."

"The boy just trying to make he grandmother happy," Sellie's father said. Rudy was silent.

"He would do better to save that money for some medicine," Mrs. Boyd said. Marcus felt like slapping her.

Sellie's father sucked his teeth loudly. "Boy, take your grandmother that food and make she feel like Christmas."

Amy Dodge looked as if she had shrunk since Marcus left home that morning. Mrs. Grace rubbed the old woman's head with a piece of cloth saturated in alcohol. She said, "Your grandmother wasn't able to drink all the soup I made."

Marcus kneeled over her cot. "Gran, how you feel?"

Her lids lay heavily over her dark eyes. "I fine. Just a little tired." Her voice sounded weak, like a wounded bird.

"I buy food for we."

"Marcus, you spend all of the money you make today?"

"Don't worry. We go' eat like it's Christmas."

"My grandson. They say you is wild, but I always know you is a good boy."

"So you going to eat this good fish and some johnnycake?"

"Yes. I going to eat it all. Just let me rest a little."

Mrs. Grace shook her head and motioned for Marcus to leave the room. "She can't eat that food. She only take a few sips from the soup I make."

"Maybe she ain't have taste for your soup."

"Sometimes me ain't know if you as fresh as you sound or your words don't come out right. Now what you going to do with all that food?"

"I going to cook it. And we is going to eat."

"Can you cook?"

"I go' learn how just now."

164

"The only good thing about you is the way you love your grandmother. I take the food home and prepare it for you."

"Why you can't fix it here?"

"I work better in me own place. I ain't go' steal your food."

Marcus swept the backyard and then showered. When he finished he went to the bedroom. Gran seemed to be getting smaller. Rivulets of perspiration trickled down her face. He put alcohol on the cloth and gently dabbed her forehead. It felt as if something in the house were choking him as he watched the only person in the world who understood and loved him drift away.

He got on his knees and buried his head in Gran's pillow. It was like when he was little and Rudy beat his behind raw. He'd run to his grandmother and bury his face in her strong arms. Now those arms were like two little sticks.

Marcus stayed where he was until Mrs. Grace returned with the food. Sellie's mother and two other women were with her. Rudy stayed in the front yard with almost half the village.

The women came into the bedroom. "We go' pray for her," they said. Marcus let them have his grandmother. Mrs. Grace had left the food on the table in the sitting room. It looked like pieces of flotsam to him now. He couldn't eat. Marcus left the house and walked past the sad faces. He felt like saying to them, Take off your funeral look, she ain't dead yet.

Marcus walked to the beach and lay down where the tide slid gently onto the white sand. The foamy edges of the waves brushed his body as he closed his eyes and attempted to cancel out his feelings.

"Marcus, get up, man. Marcus, please. Everybody worried about you."

He stared at Sellie blankly.

"Marcus, the Old Goat is there saying your granny is going to have to go to the hospital. One set of old women is praying to Jesus in your grandmother's room. And another set in the yard is lighting candles. Me mother is brewing teas and medicines."

"How is Gran?"

"She ask for you."

Sellie put his arm around Marcus's shoulders as they walked back up to St. Ann. There were still crowds of people in the front and back yards and inside the small house. Marcus walked silently to the bedroom.

"My grandson." Gran looked at the women crowding her bed. "Let me talk to my grandson." The women left.

"How you feeling, Gran?"

"Fine."

"You always say that."

"I feeling better."

"We was going to have a big dinner tonight. I buy plenty food, but you wouldn't eat."

"I go' eat some tomorrow. You a good boy, Marcus. Did you eat?"

"I waiting for you. When you eat, I eat."

"You must stay strong. You have to eat."

He propped her on the pillows. "Marcus, hear what I saying. Don't give up. You go' be a fine man. A powerful, fine man, but use your head. I know the people, them praying to this saint and praying to that god. I never tell a living soul this before." She fixed her eyes on Marcus. "I don't believe none of it. But I believe there is one thing. I love God and believe He give us the greatest gift—a brain. And since He give you a brain to use, then you don't have to be begging and crying to God all the time for help. All you need to pray

166

for is that your brain keep working, so you can think your way through life's problems."

"Gran, I see you going to church. I see you light them candles."

"Is because that's how village life is. Why should I upset the life? But your mind is your own, Marcus. People can't climb inside your head unless you invite them in."

"Gran, sometime it feel my mind go from me. When I get angry."

Her soft, frail voice wrapped itself around his body.

"Marcus, I ain't have nothing to leave you but my words. You can control your head. You know the tail don't wag the dog. You ain't some kind of wild animal to go thrashing through life. You have a mind. Use it. Don't let the world destroy you. It go' try its best—but you is special. You is a child of God and you is me and Nathaniel's grandson. And you is Louisa's and Rudy's son."

□23□

A loud crash in the outer hall woke up the old man. "What's that? Must be them junkies again."

Marcus's head throbbed. He hadn't thought about his grandmother for so long. He looked at the old man as memories of his grandmother haunted him. Then he stood up.

"Where you going, boy?"

"I don't know."

"Ain't no point in running if you don't know where you going."

Marcus went to the doorless exit. He heard feet scraping in the rubble in the outer hall and he turned to the old man. "This the only way out?"

"They ain't no way out except you know where you going." The man grinned stupidly and held the bottle up to his mouth.

Marcus was reminded of every loser he ever knew. Every old fool who couldn't give him a simple answer to a simple question. He swung around and knocked the bottle out of the man's hands. The crashing bottle and the old man's screams mingled. Someone in the hall said, "Let's get the hell out of here."

The man curled into a greasy, sobbing ball. "Why'd you do that, you little bastard? That's all I got."

Marcus hesitated at the doorway and then ran through the garbage into the street. He walked quickly down 110th Street, feeling as if he'd just made an escape from a prison. There was no point in going home. That's the first place they'd look for him. Ron's—he'd go there. No. Cassie. His father. He laughed to himself—that'd be like going to the police.

The street was quiet. He reached in his pocket and remembered that his wallet was gone. The wind seemed to push him. He heard a police siren and saw flashing lights. He ducked into a building, raced up the stairs, and passed two men coming down. They turned to look and then went on their way. He ran to the top of the steps and tried the door to the roof. It was locked.

He slumped down on the next landing. A thousand buildings in Harlem with the roofs unlocked or no doors at all, and he had to find the only one that was locked. He felt sick, as if something rotten had entered his pores. Sweat poured down his haggard face. He leaned against the banister. Instead of trying to make a plan he tried to vomit and let the sickness out of himself.

Marcus didn't hear the footsteps. But when the little girl looked at him and screamed, her voice reminded him of the child who called his name in the cane field.

□24□

A week after his grandmother had taken ill, Marcus was helping some men pile garbage on a truck. A little girl from the village ran through the workers calling for him. Her voice screeched across the fields: "Marcus, your grandmother dead. Your grandmother dead."

Everyone stopped working. Marcus heard a scream outside of himself. He whirled like the water in a pool when a pebble hits it. Large, long black arms with machetes tried to grab him. Wailing voices assaulted his ears, but he got away from them.

Marcus had no idea how long he'd been walking. He knew he was going deeper into the hills and when he heard faint drumming he followed the sound. And when he smelled wood burning he was certain he'd found the Brethren's camp.

He felt as if he were stepping inside the loud drums. Brother James had said, "When you're ready to find us you will know where to look."

"What you want, boy?" A tall man, about twenty-five, approached him. Some other Brethren stared at him.

"I come to look for Brother James."

They stared at him and he felt exposed. After a minute the man said, "There's no Brother James here."

"Brother James teach me about the Brethren. Can I stay?"

The men looked from one to the other. Finally, the tall one said, "Your vibrations is good. Stay."

About fifty men, women, and children lived in the camp. Continuous drumming and chanting filtered through a haze of blue-gray smoke. The man who said he could remain was over six feet tall, with flowing coils of hair. He led Marcus to a group of young men. They greeted him and he sat down with them on the ground.

The young men were smoking what looked like thick cigars, and the smell was pungent and sweet. The drumming, chanting, and thick smoke laced themselves around Marcus's tired body and held him there. Marcus wasn't afraid. The men didn't say anything else to him, but they were not unfriendly.

The mountains that surrounded the camp were a profound purple and seemed to hold in and protect the enclave. Marcus watched a shaft of white sunlight slide down the purple side of the mountain. One of the men handed him a thick cigar. He inhaled deeply and felt himself shrinking. Before he disappeared completely he thought he heard his grandmother call his name from one of the hills.

He woke up the following day lying on a pallet in a small, bare room. At first he didn't know where he was. Then consciousness slowly filtered back to his brain. Gran was dead and he was in a camp with the Brethren. He stepped out of the room. Even in the morning light the mountains had a purple cast. The smoke smell still hung in the cool morning air.

Some women were washing clothes in a little stream. The man who first let him into the camp sat on a stool grating coconuts. A large cooking pot of rice and peas was at his side. A young child peeled an orange and watched Marcus.

171

The man smiled at him. "You're not ready for the holy weed; you fainted yesterday. You'll be ready in time."

Marcus stayed in the camp for a week, in a dream state. The mountains were like a cocoon. The drumming and chanting drove away memories. The hazy smoke softened the sharp edges of reality. Whenever he thought back to that time afterward, he could barely recall the long, colorful dresses of the women or the little shacks that made up the compound. Instead he thought of drums, purple mountains, and a haze that covered everything—especially his mind.

On Marcus's last night at the camp the pungent smoke stung his eyes and nose more than usual. He twisted on his pallet and wondered what kind of ritual was going on. Then a brother burst into the room where he slept. "The police raiding the place!"

Marcus rolled off his pallet. He ran into the dark, smoky night. The entire camp was enveloped in screams, curses, and flames. Marcus ran, not knowing whether he was running farther into the hills or back into the arms of the pursuing police. Suddenly something connected with his head, and it felt as if his brains had exploded into the night.

Marcus looked at the empty cot where his grandmother used to sleep and wondered what he was doing there. He sat up quickly and sharp pains tore at his skull. He lay back down and fingered the bandages around his head. He looked at the empty cot again and tried to sit up once more, but the pains kept him pinned to the cot.

Rudy walked into the room. "You a fine one, Marcus. I wish they left you in the hills and never bring you back to me. You belong there in the dust." Rudy's face was twisted with grief and anger.

Marcus closed his eyes.

172

"I know you awake," Rudy continued. "Yes, look where she used to be. You ain't even come to she funeral. Your poor mother can't come, and you is here and run off. You think you is the only one who hurt?"

Marcus kept his eyes closed, but he could sense Rudy standing over him.

"Look at me, Marcus. Open them devil's eyes and look at me. I go' be your conscience now. She dead. You wasn't even at the funeral. You the most important person to she and you romping the hills with them Brethren. Open your eyes, boy. I could pelt you from one end of this room to the other now. She ain't here to protect you."

Marcus opened his eyes and stared blankly at the ceiling. A spider had spun a big web over one of the beams.

"I killing myself to get all of us off this wretched piece of island, and you up in them hills." Rudy cupped his hands around Marcus's face and forced Marcus to look at him. "The only reason I brought you back here is because the law say I still have to take care of you. When you is a man you can live any piggish way you like. But you is still a child, even though you think you is a man. You coming with me to the States. Maybe someday when you is a real man you'll have some sense and appreciate what I done for you."

□25□

"Get up. What you doing here?" The man roared like a bull. Marcus grabbed the banister and pulled himself up.

"You better get the hell out of here before I hurt you. Scaring my little girl."

As Marcus ran down the steps, the sick feeling welled up in him again. He ran uptown this time. The tenements on either side of the street seemed like giant soldiers intent on circling him until he went mad. The street was empty except for those soldier buildings hemming him in.

The flashing light of a police car streaked down the street. He jumped over the side railing of a building and crouched behind a garbage pail. When the police car had gone, Marcus climbed over the railing and raced up the avenue. The voices followed him up the street. Little girls screaming. The girls at school screaming. Cassie. Sellie. Eddie. The knife and the blood. The screams again. His grandmother. "You go' spend the rest of your life sorry over something." He had to get away from the voices.

Marcus reached 125th Street and faced a subway entrance. The train rumbling below drowned out the voices. He ran down the stairs and jumped over the turnstile. The voices came back as the train pulled off. Marcus looked down the yawning subway tunnel. Only the train could take the voices away. It could take them away forever. He looked down the tunnel again and the sick feeling returned. He saw Eddie's face contorted in pain. His eyes bulging. Blood. The wino huddled like a baby. He had to get away from the voices and the pictures in his head. The screams. The train. He'd jump in front of a train and let it make the voices and the eyes and the blood disappear.

The sick feeling filled every pore. His sour mouth trembled as he looked down the tunnel and waited for a train to come and stop the voices. He didn't know how long he waited—it could have been five minutes or five hours. Some white lights flashed on at the far end of the tunnel. The lights reminded him of carnival, when the dusty village became a place of lights and music. The lights made him think of his grandmother's candles too. He listened for her voice. Maybe it could drown out the others. He fought to find and keep her voice. "Ask God to help you keep your brain working." Her candles and her voice could destroy the bulging eyes; the blood; the screams. He fought hard to keep her voice. The lights moved closer and suddenly burst in his face.

When the doors opened he walked into the train. The car was empty. The whole train seemed empty. He felt used up and tired. But he knew now what he had to do. The train stopped at 135th Street and he didn't know whether he was going uptown or downtown. When he came to the next stop he realized that he was going uptown. He got off, crossed to the other side of the platform, and waited for the next train.

The sick feeling was gone and he felt as if he could sleep for a year. The downtown train finally came and he sat in the back of the car. He wondered what time it was. Had to be about twelve A.M. There were several people in the front

175

of the car. He sank into the seat and drifted off into a deep sleep.

"Sonny! Hey, sonny, wake up! This is the end of the line!" A short, fat conductor looked down at him. Marcus's eyes darted in confusion. "Where we?"

"Utica Avenue in Brooklyn. You could cross over to the other side if you missed your stop."

Marcus wondered why the man was being so nice to him. Why he had such a sympathetic look in his eyes. Marcus decided to walk; it was only a few blocks. He trembled as the cold seeped through his thin jacket. The block seemed narrower than it had the last time he was there. The stoop was empty. Where were the police with guns drawn? Marcus ran up the four flights of stairs and banged on the door.

When Rudy opened the door his gray Afro seemed to stand straight up in a wild bush. His bloodshot eyes stared at Marcus for a second. Marcus steeled himself for the blow. Rudy's fist crashed into his face and pummeled his head, chest, and back. Marcus fell silently to the floor without trying to protect himself or fight back. No shouts, screams, or words passed between them. Only the sounds of Rudy's fists hammering on Marcus's body and the soft thud when he fell down.

A neighbor opened and closed her door quickly. Rudy pulled Marcus into the apartment and pushed him down onto a kitchen chair. Rudy stood at the other end of the table and breathed heavily.

Marcus stared at him blankly. "Go on, Daddy. Kill me."

Rudy opened his mouth but nothing came out. He sat across from Marcus and covered his face with his hands. Marcus stared at Rudy's gnarled, worn hands, which seemed to have nothing to do with his handsome features. Marcus some of it must have been pride. When a man have nothing but foolish pride, he'll do anything for it."

Marcus fell into a fitful doze. When they were leaving the East River Drive and entering the Bronx the sound of his name jolted him awake. Rudy was calling him. He felt his father's hard, calloused hand cover his and stiffened at the strangeness of Rudy's touch. Marcus didn't move his hands and slowly the unnaturalness he felt at Rudy's attempt to comfort went away.

"I moving back to the Bronx," Rudy said. "No man can break up a family. Is like saying you don't want your mother to be your mother no more. Or your son to be your son. It's a thing you can't change. It's all you have in this world."

Louisa was at the precinct when they got there. She held Marcus for a long time and said, "It go' be all right, Marcus." He was surprised that she seemed so calm. But she gripped his hand tightly as the three of them sat together on a long bench.

When Marcus was called to the desk, he kissed Louisa. She looked at him and then at Rudy. Marcus made a slight movement toward his father, but didn't complete it. He said, "Daddy, Mommy, pray for that boy I hurt. Pray for Ron and me. Pray for all us boys."

Rudy moved closer to him. Marcus flinched slightly as if he were expecting a blow. "I praying for everyone, Marcus. Including us."

When Marcus felt Rudy's strong arms embracing him he was moved in a way he'd never before experienced. Now he could say the thing that needed saying. Sorry wasn't enough.

"Daddy . . ."

Rudy let him go and looked at him closely. "Yes, Marcus?"

"I love you."

ABOUT THE AUTHOR

Joyce Hansen grew up in the Bronx, and presently lives in New York City where she teaches school. While writing *Home Boy*, she remembered the stories that her father told her of his life as a boy in the Virgin Islands, and later as a young man in Harlem, and many of them became a part of the story.

Home Boy is Ms. Hansen's second novel. His first was *The Gift-Giver*, which *Kirkus Reviews* described as: "An unusually alive, unforced story of black inner-city life . . . It puts universal feelings in a fresh perspective—quite apart from its implicit inducement to cope and conquer."

SEP 2 5 2014